BOOK ONE

CANDY MAN

JAS T. WARD

BOOK ONE: CANDYMAN
The Grid Series

For Information, address:
Ink-N-Flow Publishing
www.AuthorJasTWard.com
hello@AuthorJasTWard.com

Cover Design: T.E.Black Designs

Two Red Pens Editing
Colleen Snibson, Chief Editor
Helen Mitchell, Proofreader
Rogena Mitchell-Jones
Literary Editor
Courtney Shockey, Libra Formatting

THE GRID SERIES READING ORDER:

A WORD ABOUT CANDYMAN

What can I say about Reno Sundown who you met in Madness? He is by far my most favorite of voices. And if you are here to learn his history before the Madness, welcome.

He was created as a voice, literally in a character's head, but he made an impact from the first moment he spoke.

The fans loved him, and it was that love for the Candyman (as his fans called him in the fan-fiction world) that created him and the Shadow-Keepers series.

He was never supposed to be—both literary wise and literally—as I had plans for killing him off and silencing that voice. But fans of my writing went insane to the point I got hate mail and angry comments on my social media sites if I dared to do it.

So, Twiz (my creative, writing muse/demon) and I got together and created a life of Reno's own. And it was inspiration hidden in an effort to please.

But through it all, so much had taken place with the character that I had to trim it all down, adapt it to stand on its own, and weave a whole new world. It would have been impossible to put into one book, so I decided, as a gift of gratitude to the readers that wanted this collection, I would place his backstory here, in the form of a novella, and start his book with his new existence. T following is that backstory, which is from Reno's point of view as only he could tell it. In his book, Madness, he allows me to tell the story.

I love Reno. He's the side of me that I wish I could be twenty-four seven, but life has a way of making you be who you need to be, not who you want to be. For those who haven't met Reno, I invite you to dive right in and learn what never taking for granted is all about, standing up for what you believe is yours, and laughing and crying, all at the same time.

To those who do know and love Reno Sundown, who used to be the dark half of a personality in a hero's head, here it is. Enjoy. And thank you for making sure his voice was heard.

- JTW

This book was originally included in the fan-appreciation collection of Jas T. Ward's by the name of Bits and Pieces: Tales and Sonnets, *published by Dead Bound Publishing and released in April of 2013.*

PROLOGUE

Sundown—a.k.a. Split.

And later, but you don't know that yet, Reno Sundown. But I'm getting ahead of myself. I do that. A lot, a lot.

Is that complicated enough? Keep reading.

If you had to ask me what I am, well, it's kinda complicated, but here we go.

I'm old. But not really.

I'm nice. But deadly.

I'm light. And I'm dark.

I love candy—a good thing, too, since I need it to calm my head down. Makes the disorientation of what I am to become seem less scary. So much so that in the future, I'll be called Candyman. Oops, I got ahead of our story again, didn't I. I did warn you, though. Sorry.

I can control bad things, and I can do good things. And all of that is just my daily to-do list.

Maybe we should do this the way the fairy tales do. I love those, don't you? So here goes—

Once upon a time, there was a boy. Just a little boy, nothing special and nothing really different about him. Or so people thought. What they and the little boy didn't know was that he had a destiny to fulfill. An ancient prophecy since the beginning of time, which would be coming true in about one hundred and fifty years.

Although this kid didn't know, others knew, and they wanted to stop that prophecy from coming true. So they hunted down this little boy even though he didn't know why. His own family threw him out into the wilderness of the Old West, and that was another thing he didn't understand. He knew his mom couldn't help it, she kinda died, but his father? Totally didn't get that one.

So here was this little boy with this big destiny laid out in front of him, and he wasn't going to last the night. That's where I came in.

CHAPTER ONE

Hi! I'm in your head

The first thing that told me I was alive was the grass under my feet. Weird, I know. But it was cool, wet grass coated with dew on that summer night. I had not a thought before, yet here it was— grass.

The next thing was a shot. Yep, a gun blast right between those same feet and one word screamed out in our head. *Run!*

But the kid didn't listen, and as much as I screamed it, the kid just stood there and stared down the barrel of that pistol, crying and sobbing, begging his father not to do it. Had to feel sorry for the kid; his mother had just died, and his father wanted him dead. Not exactly a shining moment to come into the big picture.

But maybe it was the perfect time as the kid was paralyzed with fear, loss, and pain.

Meet William Jess Bailey, who goes by Jess because he hated being a junior to his asshole father. Scrawny kid, and remember that whole destiny rushing toward a kid thing? Yep, that kid.

Who was about to be coyote food if I didn't do something fast. Another shot rang out, and the ranch hands, as drunk as Jess's father, all laughed, and Jess just stood there crying. Talk about harsh, man. The Old West was harsh.

But more about that later.
Where was I?

Oh, yeah.

So anyway...

Kid, we really, really need to move.

Nothing. So I took matters into my own hands. Well, if I had any hands. His would just have to do. His feet, too, I guess.

That was the first time I became the driver. What's a driver you ask? Oh well, see, it's kind of like a clown car. But uh, no clowns. Just me, and Jess, and... well, Madness. But we'll talk about that later. Anyway, one of us has to be in charge of the body like the car. Otherwise, it just kind of crashes and takes out porta-potties and innocents.

Apparently, Jess was not able to drive, so the next thing I knew, not only did I feel that grass under my feet but I could control those feet, too. And control I did. We ran—fast. And even then, more shots rang out, chasing us into the desert of West Texas, deep into the wilderness.

I don't know how far we ran, but we ran until our bare feet were cut and bloodied, our lungs were on fire, and we ran out of tears to cry. Landing hard on our knees, I stared at the rocks and sand, my breath coming out hard and fast when I first heard the voice in our head.

Who are you?

I looked up. Hmm... how to answer that one? I really wasn't sure. But I knew I had a purpose, a reason to be here, and this little boy was it. "Uh, I don't have a name. Not really." I rolled to sit, pulling up our legs, knees to chest, resting my chin on a boney, cut-up knee.

What are you?

Another good question. Wish I had a good answer. Sighing, I thought about that and looked at the night around us. "I'm part of you. Or I am now. And I've been sent here to make sure you're okay. To help you and stuff."

Our head grew silent for a few minutes.

Sent by who?

Okay, I could tell who the smarter of the two of us was, and it wasn't me. Shrugging, I said, "I know, but I don't know. It's kind of weird like it's not time yet. I guess we'll find out when we need to."

I'm scared.

"I am, too. But we'll do this together, okay? I think that's what we're supposed to do."

Okay. Can I stay in here for a while?

That right there would set the trend for our time together. See, I was sent to handle the bad, the painful, and the most horrible that might come back this kid's way. So he could meet his destiny, and he would survive. Doesn't seem so bad, right?

Just wait. It gets worse.

CHAPTER TWO

I'm not bad, just misunderstood

So, the part where it got worse?

Wait for it. It's coming—promise.

Jess survived that night, and we got to town. I learned a crucial thing that night, and so did he.

He was in charge, and I was not. As soon as we hit the town, and he calmed down, he came out, and I went in.

It shouldn't have been that big of a deal, right? It's not like I was real, I was just a splintered half of a destined hero, used to handle the bad and the pain so he could survive. After all, he had the heart, the soul, and compassion.

I don't think I had any of those. Or was supposed to have. Then.

Wait, getting ahead of ourselves. I do that. Sorry.

We lived on the streets, and the Old West wasn't like what you would call it now. They beat you and kicked you, and no one cared. You were the same level as a stray dog in those times. But, somehow, we survived. I didn't come out much, except when Jess got beat up too bad.

Then I got to have some fun. Because I loved to fight, which almost made me feel empowered, stronger, and I learned I could stay out longer. As long as I was fighting, inflicting and taking the pain, I remained the driver.

Valuable information right there—did you

make a note of that? In fact, get a big pad because this is going to get complicated. I like blue ink myself, just looks cooler, especially if you have one of those yellow pads. It makes the ink look kind of green.

Wait. I did it again. I rambled. Sorry, I do that, too—a lot.

So, Old West, getting beaten up a lot, and learning what I could and couldn't do.

The thing with learning is that he was learning, too. And not just about how he could pull me back in as he calmed down but new skills, as well. Jess was a charmer, good with words and able to have people trust him pretty easily.

All in all? Jess was a good kid, who just happened to have a really bad side. Enter me—the bad side.

Oh, wait, you don't know my name. See, I told you he had all the manners.

My name now is Reno. Yes, I know, like the town. But remember, we're trying not to get too far ahead. Back then, I went by the name that Jess decided. It meant going from the light of day to the dark of night, representing the time when bad things happened in Jess's mind—his mother died and being tossed out into the night.

So he gave me the name Sundown.

Pretty cool, huh?

Jess learned to deal around town and stay out of trouble. Good for him, but not so good for me. So I would go into a kind of suspended animation, I guess you could call it. Days, weeks, months would go by, and I would not know a thing. Some days, I stirred and rattled and sat there, blankly staring at walls that weren't there like a void in Jess's psyche. Most of the time, I just wanted to go back to not being there. It was better than the boredom, the anxiety of worrying if I was never going to get out again.

The resentment that was starting to build.

You know that saying, be careful what you wish for? Yeah, that one.

Well, that summer, we met the Preacher Man. And that summer changed it all. Here comes that worse stuff.

CHAPTER THREE

Save your soul

Sundown, *I don't think this is smart.*

Hearing Jess, I rolled my eyes as I looked at the playground. We were once again locked up in the county orphanage after being told that it would save our soul and teach us some skills. At this point, the only skills we were learning were how to avoid the Preacher Man's fist and not starve day-to-day while the Preacher Man got fatter, meaner, and lazier.

I was hoping for the lazy part as we watched him sleeping under the shade of an old cedar tree, one greasy hand holding a biscuit while the other held a jug of shine. "I know, Jess. But I don't want belly being the loudest voice in this mix, either."

My eyes were trained on that basket of biscuits, my mouth watering at the open jar of strawberry jam sitting to the side, small fists clenching at our side. It seemed pretty easy as my eyes darted around the playground—if you could call it that. It was nothing but dirt, sand, and one single busted swing, littered with old whiskey barrels.

The rest of the kids had given up and just sat in the little shade there was, trying to make it to the one meal we got a day. And sometimes all that consisted of was watered-down stew with no meat and just taters and turnips—rotted ones if we were unlucky that day. Most of the kids were sick and beaten and just waiting to die.

I couldn't let that happen. I had to protect Jess.

It was part of my purpose, and without him, I don't think I would be around, either. So I was kind of selfish on the not dying thing. And no way did I want it happening here. Or anywhere.

The Preacher Man fell asleep, and as the precious biscuit hit the dirt with a soft thud, every single kids' eyes went to that small piece of half-eaten bread. But none of them would act on it. They were smart.

I was just hungry.

As I bunched up our skinny legs and took off, leaping over a barrel, all eyes were trained on me while I had mine fixed on that basket of biscuits. Had to be a dozen in that basket, and there were a dozen of us. I would keep that jar of jam for myself. I was developing this weird need for something sweet. It made my head feel…I don't know, different. And something told me that was important.

Just another one of those we'll-find-out-eventually things. I make a note of everything when it's important.

The rest, uh, I usually forget.

Oh yeah, see, warned you. I ramble.

I know if those kids could have cheered they would have when my hands latched on to that basket of biscuits, scooping low and silent to grab the handle. I spun on my heels and ran into the shadows to pass them out. I was feeling pretty victorious for about three seconds until I felt a greasy, meaty hand grab my wrist and spin me around.

Well, see, remember that not smart thing? This was one of those moments.

"What the hell are you doing, Bailey?" The Preacher Man's eyes darted from my brown ones to that basket of biscuits and back up again. "Are you stealing from the Lord?"

I thought about that one. There were probably a dozen better ways to answer it, and Jess was pleading in my head to back down.

Sundown! Please! Don't!

But instead of listening and being smart—as established, I was not the smart side—I said, "No, just you. I wouldn't dare steal from the Lord. I hear he's a nice fella."

Have you ever been backhanded? Let me tell you, smarts worse than any whooping and makes your head ring like a bell. But that's what it got me. It wasn't the first, and it wouldn't be the last.

I spun to the ground. Dust flew up, and the biscuits became airborne as I hit, blood filling our mouth with its coppery taste. Then there was a spurt of power, and I jumped up fast. The Preacher Man blinked as I put my fist up, ready to fight. We had hit our limit. Okay, I had. Jess was still begging me to back down. He does that.

He does that—a lot.

"Are you trying to fight me, boy? The one that is trying to save your soul? I'm a servant of the Lord. Have you no respect?"

Ha, I didn't have a soul. Well, okay, maybe half of one. And it hadn't really done much for us at this point, so I wasn't sure that saving it was worth the effort.

I smirked, small hands balled up tightly into fists. "Not for you. You're a lousy servant. And you keep your paws off our soul."

I jabbed hard, and it didn't do much of anything. Fat is like, I don't know, body armor or something if you're a little kid of seven.

He laughed and backhanded me again. And

once again, Jess was screaming in our head for me to stop. But he knew I couldn't. Right back to that purpose thing. This was what I did. This was how I survived.

I went berserk. See, pain does this weird thing to me. Makes everything go red and bright, and it almost slowed things down. Like I can step back, take a look, decide what to do next, and do it. It's really cool. But uh, not so good for our body.

I leaped at the Preacher Man and scrambled onto his back. By now, the other kids were up on their feet, cheering and screaming, urging me on. For that moment, I was a hero. And it was something I had never felt before.

And I liked it.

Preacher Man stumbled and bellowed, trying to get me off his back. I was like some crazed monkey as I clawed at his neck—I even bit his ear, ripping off a hunk—and started punching. I just wanted him gone. I wanted the pain and fear he put into every little kid who was watching in awe to be felt in every single punch my little fists could pound.

But I was just that, a little kid, and it didn't take long before Preacher Man grabbed me and was able to rip me free and throw me hard against the wood plank fence. So hard I heard something crack while something else ripped, and I saw stars. But I didn't care. I wanted that pain. It meant I could finish the job.

The Preacher Man approached, all huffed and bleeding, and kicked us twice, three times, and I felt something else pop as I grabbed his ankle and wrapped myself around it, only to get punched in the head.

Ouch. Forget the backhand, getting punched in the head hurts big time and kinda took me out of the game.

As I lay there dazed, my eyes went to the biscuits, covered in dirt and sand, some of them smashed in the fight. I was just hungry. And as the Preacher Man picked me up by the back of my neck to drag me to the Hand of the Lord—a.k.a. the small locked closet in the back of the chapel—I saw kids scramble to pick up those biscuits, not caring for the dirt and the dust, and then watch, once again, with eyes filled with awe.

And I smiled. I liked that feeling. I liked it—a lot.

CHAPTER FOUR

A hero is born

"Jess?"

I wanted to say, "No. Sorry, Jess isn't here right now. He's too hurt and beat up to come out and play." But then I looked up and saw who it was, and all thoughts flew right out the cracks in those lousy wooden walls.

She was tiny, just a little bit of a girl. We were the same age, but whereas Jess seemed to thrive via me in this environment, the other kids weren't so lucky. She was skinny, and her hair was black as a raven's wing. But her eyes, god, her eyes were like heaven. They were a deep hazel flecked with blue, and I thought that had to be what the sky looked like above where the Lord lived. And I wanted to go there, just to dive into those hazel depths for a little while.

"Jess?" she said again as I opened my cracked and busted lips to speak and only a croak came out. Three days locked up in a cramped little closet in the New Mexico summer heat with no food or water kinda takes its toll. Add to that being beaten half to Sunday, and I had to be a bad sight.

"Yeah?" Hey, looky there, a word. Genius, charmer, that's you, Sundown.

She sank to the ground and sat, pulling her ragtag dress over her knees as she drew them up, her bare feet dirty and yet still so pretty. I wanted to touch them and her hands, which looked so slender and gentle. And her hair—I bet it was soft and maybe even smelled good.

That was when something amazing happened, life-changing when you looked back at it. She held out that jar of jam. "I saved this for you. Sorry, all the biscuits got took. But no one saw this."

My eyes went to that small jar, which she had wrapped a piece of paper and ribbon around the top to keep out the flies, and something inside of me just changed. No one had ever given me anything. No one had even thought I needed anything. No one even knew I existed. As my eyes met hers, I ignored the fact that she didn't know I existed, either. She thought I was Jess.

They all did.

They thought Jess had done the hero thing, had taken on the man who tortured them all. That normally didn't bother me, but for some reason, from her, it did. I frowned looking at that cracked, days old jam and nodded, reaching out to take it.

"Thanks."

She nodded, tilting her head. "Jess? It doesn't make you happy? I'm sorry. I thought it would."

I looked up and met those beautiful hazel eyes and smiled at her. "Nah. It makes me happy. Thanks. I'm just…" *not who you think I am. I wish I was.* And something else bloomed inside our little boy heart. "… not okay right now."

Resentment. Need. Jealously. Envy and bitterness.

If only I had known there was so much more because we were no longer alone. But we didn't know that then. Gosh, I wish I had.

CHAPTER FIVE

And it all went bad

"**I** want to kiss her."

Jess had healed and weeks had passed. I behaved for the most part and looked at what Jess was looking at.

Sometimes he would let me watch what he did like a backseat driver in his head.

Her. The little girl. My heaven.

I panicked as I felt something weird twisting and turning, and before I could stop myself, I said, *No.*

Jess paused. I could feel it—the frown and the smirk. "Why?"

I floundered for words as I watched her sitting there in the sun, drawing little pictures of flowers in the dirt where they would never stand a chance of growing. What could I tell him? Did he know? No way had he known. He'd been too hurt, too deep. Did I show him that day when she gave me the jam? The empty jar I still had hidden in the floorboard under our pallet, wrapped with that piece of ribbon from her dark hair. No, I was sure of it.

Which meant only one thing.

He wanted what I wanted. Twist, coil, turn. Twist, coil, turn. *No!*

But it was too late. Jess was on his feet and walking into that bright sunny day toward my Heaven, and she looked up and smiled.

"Hi."

He smiled as I watched helpless, seeing worship in her eyes, worship that should have been mine. Eyes that should only look into mine. If I had my own eyes.

But I didn't, and she didn't know that the little boy she had given the jam to was silently pleading for her to reject her hero, the one who stood in front of her. To somehow sense they weren't the same. To know he was there inside and to know he wanted so badly to be outside.

Jess went to his knees and said a soft "Howdy."

She smiled so sweetly, and all I could do was watch. That was supposed to be *my* smile. It was supposed to be for *me*. Not him.

Jess. Please, no.

I should look away. Not watch. But I couldn't. Note that... because it's a bitch for me for a long time.

They talked, and she laughed, and then he said words that told me nothing in my existence was private. It was all up for grabs with him.

"Thanks for the jam."

She smiled more and nodded. "You did a really nice thing."

Not him. *Me!* Not Jess, *me!* I did a nice thing. Please feel that. Please!

Jess nodded. "Well, maybe." He met her eyes and gave a shy smile. "I was wondering, can I give you a kiss to thank you for it? A little one?"

That crushed me, and I threw my fists against the little mind space I existed in. The words, *Please don't,* screamed from my lips, but he ignored me. I know he heard me. He just didn't care. He just wanted what I couldn't have.

She's mine. Please, Jess. Don't kiss her!

Please!

She looked down, playing with the hem of her pale yellow dress then looked around them. The playground was just kids. The Preacher Man always slept the hottest part of the day away while he threw the kids in the locked, fenced area. She looked back up and giggled and nodded.

No. Please! No!

Jess smiled and leaned forward, my screams sounding to the walls of our mind. She closed her eyes and then...

I felt the gentle brush of her lips, softer than velvet, against mine as I blinked. It was my eyes looking at her eyelashes brushing the curves of her cheek. It was my hand that came up and brushed fingers along her jaw, skin so soft it didn't seem real. The kiss was innocent like nothing I had ever felt before, so sweet, so tender. It was our first kiss.

No, it was mine and only mine, I realized. It was me she was kissing. How?

Her eyes came open, fluttering like a moth, and she looked into my eyes as her brows came down a bit as if she could tell something had changed. As she pulled back—I didn't dare to move—she tilted her head and whispered, "It's you."

"How—"

But before I could finish, a bellow came from the small hut in the corner as Preacher Man rushed toward us.

Heaven jumped up, letting out a cry of alert. "Run! Run!"

But it was too late as he grabbed me by the throat and shook me like a rag doll, toes far above the ground. Heaven cried out and ran over, slapping her hands against the Preacher Man, begging him to let me go, and he backhanded her.

I roared out, but no sound came as his hand had a painful lock around my throat. I slammed my fist against his face, blood spurting after a half-dozen blows as he beat me. He reared back a meaty fist and hit me in the face for the third time, and I sagged, my eyes rolling back just seconds after the last thing I saw.

Eyes like heaven, full of tears. Tears for me. Not him.

Me.

CHAPTER SIX

Split and goodbye good

I came to, blinking and trying to clear my head, to the sounds of crying. I hurt all over and knew I was still out while Jess was still in. When I lifted my head, that was when I saw it. And god, I wished I hadn't.

Heaven was the one crying. And she was crying because the Preacher Man was doing bad things. Things that no little girl should have to know or feel. Rage rose, and the room went too bright as I got to my hands and knees.

"Stop."

Was that my voice? It sounded strange like it had something there that was layered and dark.

Preacher Man stopped, stood, and looked over his shoulder to sneer at us. "Well, you still alive? Ain't that remarkable. God be praised."

Heaven was crying and tried to crawl away. Her torn dress barely covered her small frame, and her thin arms tried to cover her bareness. I needed to get her out of here, but the Preacher Man stood between her, me, and the door.

That whole being punched in the head thing? It leaves your brain feeling like it's wrapped in flannel, but when Preacher Man grabbed Heaven and made her scream? That flannel shredded, and I was up on my feet. Everything went red again, and I jumped on him like some rabid demon and just started clawing and punching.

The big man staggered back, and I screamed for Heaven to run, get out, but she didn't. She just crawled to the corner and curled up, knees to chest, and wrapped her arms around her.

Great. But I guess if I were her, I would have done it, too. I really wish she hadn't. Worse? Yeah, you'll see.

Anyway, Preacher Man stumbled and tried to grab me, but I was in the total you-need-to-stop-and-be-gone mode. He got hold of one of my arms and threw me across the room. Slowed me down for about a second, but I was right back at kicking and punching, using his belly rolls like a ladder to latch on and punch his head.

I took some hits because I tasted blood in my mouth, heard ringing in my head, and had a burning in my chest. And I didn't feel a thing. Pain was becoming something I would not acknowledge. In fact, it seemed to fuel me on. That would be an issue, too, in the future.

But I couldn't seem to stop even when Preacher Man crashed to the floor. The whole shack trembled with the impact, and I rolled off only to go into a crouch and growl.

Growl? That was new. But that's something I'll do a lot of, too. *A lot* a lot.

Preacher Man was struggling to get that great mass off the floor, and Heaven was crying and screaming. Jess was pleading for us to run.

And all I wanted to do? Bet you can guess. It's pretty easy. Get revenge.

As Preacher Man got to his knees, I ran and grabbed the spittoon by the bed, splattering the room and me with nasty, brown spit and tobacco, and swung it. Once, twice, and a third time.

Strength bloomed and flowed, from where, I had no idea, but I used every bit of it in those swings. So much so, that on the last one, Preacher Man's head split like an overripe melon, causing him to suddenly stop moving and just fall. It was kinda like watching a giant stubby tree go down.

He hit the small wood-burning stove, and it overturned, breaking free from the stove pipe and sending a cloud of black soot and ash into the air.

Heaven screamed, and I whipped around and held out my hand. "Come on! We have to get out of here!"

Thinking back on it now, I must have been the sight one sees in a nightmare—covered in blood, both the Preacher Man's and mine with black ash clinging to the sweat. No wonder she just screamed and pointed at me to stay back, go away, like you would a monster.

Because I was one or was becoming one.

I tried to get her to go. I needed her to go as flames licked up the shabby walls of that shack and overtook Preacher Man's body, putting out a sickening stench with horrible popping noises.

"Please, come with me. I'm okay now. I'd never hurt you!"

Heaven just screamed and screamed. It was horrible, and it made something hurt in my chest. Something sad and tragic. But the place was coming down around us, burning pieces falling and one landed on the trailing scrap of her dress. She saw it and looked at me.

And for a moment, one that was too late, there was pure and simple clarity. Shame that moment didn't come before the place started crashing around us.

Sundown. Run*! It's too late. Get us out of here!*

"No! I can save her. I have to save her!"

I tried getting past the burning beam that had crashed down. The walls were on fire, everything was on fire, and I burned my hands as I grabbed debris, trying to get to Heaven.

But what I found? Heaven was no longer heaven but a piece of hell. Face contorted in pain as she was engulfed in flames. Those eyes would never give me a glimpse of where angels flew again.

I staggered away from the sight and considered just sitting there. It would be painful—already our skin smoked and blisters bubbled, and our hair was crisp and burnt—but it would be over.

For Jess.

For me.

Just done.

Make a note of that because this won't be the first time I have those kinda thoughts.

Sundown, please. I know. But remember your purpose?

That got to me. As bitter and rebellious as I wanted to be, my purpose still drove me. Drove me so well that we made it out seconds before the structure collapsed in a burning heap. It took no time for burning embers to alight on the other buildings and set them on fire. Kids came running and screaming, some of them going to the same burning hell as Heaven.

A hell I made.

We once again ran, and when we did, we sealed our fate. Any dreams Jess had of a normal, happy life were over and done.

At the age of seven, we were now a wanted murderer. For the death of one Preacher and half a dozen children, as well as burning down the orphanage. All witnessed by the lonely cook, who knew about her husband's depravity with children and never did a thing.

Yeah, the Old West was brutal. And it was about to find a new legend for that brutality. Usher in... the hired gun.

CHAPTER SEVEN

Hot lead and out

Jess kept me put away for a long time after that. Which was fine because I found out it takes a long time to heal from a blow to the heart. So long that time was a blur.

Next thing I knew, or cared, we were sixteen years old and members of a gang. Not a hip-hop gang, though that would have been both cool and funny in the Old West, but a bank-robbing gang, and trains, and hired deeds, and just an all-around "you pay and it's done" kinda gang.

It was led by Zack; whose background was about as tragic as ours. But unlike Jess, who had this never-defeated good guy side that he kept buried under a cowboy hat and a smile, Zack didn't. Not that we ever saw.

Zack was in his mid-forties and tried to be a father figure we never had. He failed almost ninety percent of the time, but it was more than Jess's real father had pulled off. Jess idolized Zack and would do whatever the man asked.

Zack realized early on there was something special about Jess. He never missed a shot even with his eyes closed. And no one fought more brutally and deadly than Jess when cornered. You can thank me for that last part. But that was our secret and not one that Jess wanted anyone to know about.

By this time, that resentment, anger, and hate that started after the orphanage fire, which ruined

Jess' life and ended Heaven's, were fully grown into something that had us not liking each other very much. It was pretty bad when your worst enemy shared the same body, the same life, and the same destiny.

See? Told you—complicated.

It's a bad idea, Jess. Zack doesn't care, and even you can see it's a really, really bad idea.

I knew he wasn't going to listen to me. He almost never did anymore. Now I only came out if I was needed.

And with the current lifestyle choice?

I came out a lot.

But Jess and I hadn't worked together as friends since that horrible day at the orphanage. Not only the children whose lives were ruined or tragically lost in that fire but the trust and faith he had in his best friend.

Me.

Zack wanted Jess to lead the gang into town on a stagecoach robbery. Something about how Zack talked about the ease of the job had all kinds of bells and whistles going off in our head. But Jess was ignoring them and me.

It seemed easy since we had done dozens of hits. Taken more money than the richest rancher, more than probably Jess's father, but Zack still wanted more. So the old man always insisted on running the jobs himself.

Until this one. Why? And why wasn't Jess asking that harder than he was?

"Okay. So we go in, grab and shoot, and it's that easy?"

Zack smiled, lighting up a hand-rolled cigarette. "Yep. Just ride in, do what you do best, and

I'll be waiting right here."

Why isn't he going, Jess? He always goes. Come on. You're smarter than this. You are making my purpose pretty difficult nowadays. Listen to me, dammit!

Jess shut me out, shaking his head, his gaze returning to the town. He was listening to me, I could tell, he just wasn't going to do anything other than what he wanted to do, at all.

To prove that he could. Without me.

Oh, great. Pride, you suck. Really, really hard. And I knew that pain was soon coming our way.

Fine. Tell you what. You be all stupid, and I'll just sit here and wait to take the bad. It's all I'm good for, right?

That probably got me one big ole smirk with a side order of yep tossed in. Nothing new there

The others gathered, all raring to go, and I just sat back and watched. What else could I do? No way could I be the driver unless Jess got hurt, wounded, or pissed off. None of which he was now.

Wished stupid was on that list. Guess I was the smarter one sometimes.

We rode into town, a typical quiet, sleepy town. Which would seem nice, but when you didn't have electricity like they didn't back then, daytime was when you got stuff done.

Jess, come on. Even you gotta feel it.

That got me a hiss, so I shut up. I do that. Sometimes.

The bank was small just like the town, and just like the town, quiet. Tying up the horses, all the gang made their way to the bank, and Jess, as always, went in last. See, we had this thing about people being behind us. Just a peeve really.

Or so we thought.

Chris was the first one to say, "Robbery, folks. Hands up."

Okay, so it was all going well—until we felt it.

By then it was too late.

The bullet burned as it cut a path across our side, chipping a rib. Jess didn't even hesitate, and I was itching to come out. That rage rose higher and higher, a high just waiting to hit. Another shot rang out, this time seeking Jess as the bullet shattered the glass, and he was firing back. This one tunneled through our upper arm.

And it hurt. Bad. Which was good for me.

Do it. Come on. Do it!

Suddenly, I was out, and the grin that spread on our face was amused, happy, and deadly as fuck. I didn't hesitate as I stood to fire then kicked the door open, stepping out into the sun.

It had been a setup, which was obvious by the posse on the roofs, behind the porches, and in the shadows. Growling, I fired shot after shot. Bodies dropped from the roofs as I yelled back, "Get out here. Now!"

The boys came pouring out, sporting more wounds but still walking and firing behind us. The horses were tugging on their reins, frantic to get out of there as much as we were. We got to them but not before we took one more shot to the leg, this one making me sag forward.

And pissing me off—a lot. That is a real big problem. Don't worry. I learn to deal. Well, sorta.

I stood there, blood pouring and hitting the hot wooden plank sidewalk, before stepping off into the street and getting a line of sight, ignoring the calls for the gang to go.

"Let's go, Jess. Come on!"

I fired. And kept firing. I didn't care if it was posse or scurrying bystander. Innocent or guilty. I just wanted to hurt.

Sundown! Dammit. Stop. Let's go!

"He set us up. Dammit. They need to fucking pay!"

They didn't do it. Now stop. Please!

I blinked and dropped my arms, guns smoking, empty shells hot at my feet. Reaching back, I grabbed the saddle horn, swung myself into the saddle, and mounted up.

More than two dozen died that day. Almost all done by bullets with JB carved into the brass. But it was me who pulled the trigger, and the blood would be on my hands. If I had any. So Jess staining his would have to do.

CHAPTER EIGHT

It just keeps getting worse

Zack had nothing to say about what happened when we returned to camp. Just counted the money, counted the men lost as part of the life, and sad to say, laughed at me when I tried to get him to say it was a setup. Yeah, I was never the one good at talking.

Things kept going okay for a while. We robbed some banks, then trains, and kept getting richer and richer—until Jess met her.

Meg. Lovely, beautiful, sweet, blonde, blue-eyed Meg. She was the shopkeeper's daughter, and Jess saw her one day when we rode into town for supplies. And that was the very beginning of the end.

Well, of the first one.

"Jess, you're talking stupid. Give it all up? You're fucking kidding, right?"

Jess had been trying to convince Zack for days that he was done—done with the lifestyle, done with being a hired gun, just done.

Why? Yep. You guessed it. Her. So done that he was planning on asking Meg to marry him, buying a hunk of land, and becoming a farmer. Yeah, I kinda blinked at that one, too. But he was dead set on making it happen.

And Zack was dead set on making sure it didn't.

I was on Zack's side. What can I say? Romance at that time was not what I considered wise.

Don't worry. That changes. But don't think it was for the better. What would be the fun in that?

"Zack, I'm giving you the gang. Hell, I'm even giving you most of the cash. Apart from enough to get started, you can have it all."

Zack gave him a dark stare. "We ain't anything without your skills. You're the best gun we have. And the men like you. Hell, I've treated you like a damn son."

Jess sighed and looked down at the sand under our boots, torn up so bad that even I felt the pain of it. Zack really was the father we never had, abusive or not. But Jess had it bad for Meg, so much so that he truly believed what he was saying. And the next day, he just walked away from it all.

Shame Zack didn't let him get that far.

CHAPTER NINE

Bye-bye

The first thing that registered? Fear. The next thing? Pain. And after that? Rage. The bullet went in through the back of us and out through the front. White-hot, sizzling pain that spun us around only to get shot a second time, this one shattering our rib cage and making the first pain feel like a paper cut.

The ground came up fast, and our jaw hit the ground, shattering bone and breaking teeth. But the pain was a trigger, and rage was a bullet, too. I shot to the front in one desperate play to live.

Zack fired another shot as I rose to our feet snarling, blood running down my bottom lip and dripping off my chin to join the splattering of our blood on the ground. Zack's eyes went wide in shock, staring at his gun like he doubted its integrity. I took that chance to rush the older man, slamming him facedown into the sandy, gritty ground.

My vision turned red, flipping to a glaring and enraged zone as I lifted Zack's head and slammed it again and again and again. The sand around us darkened with crimson, turning black as Zack's skull shattered, skin and muscle shredding, and yet I couldn't stop.

Only after there was nothing left to crush, smash, or destroy of Zack's head did I stop and rise to my feet. But we were hurt—bad. All that blood in the sand? Wasn't only Zack's blood.

I made it about five steps before my vision went full of black spots and streaks, and I staggered as I tried to grab the horse's saddle horn to haul myself up. I should have sensed the other threat waiting in the shadows to take advantage of the situation. Someone who wanted the bounty but did not want to get his hands dirty. Another shot fired, and I never made it up into the saddle. Instead, we hit the blood-soaked dirt. The sun was blazing hot, yet I seemed so cold as I whispered in our head, *I'm sorry, Jess. Looks like I failed. She's better off without us anyway.*

The very last images our flickering brain registered were expensive black boots and a strangely friendly smile right before an uninvited bullet fired and joined us in our brain.

CHAPTER TEN

Immortality sucks

I never signed up for the hero part. That was all Jess.

See, here's the deal. There are powers at work that we can't and will never understand. Seems like when you have value in one life, you have value in someone else's, and if you're dead? You're kind of up for grabs.

So Jess signed up for undead hero time, working for an immortal, ancient god called Bounce, who enlisted individuals with, how can I say this, colorful pasts.

Wait! That word isn't right.

Indentured, enslaved and bound you into duty to do the better good for mankind. To hunt down, eradicate, and rid the world of bad things.

Bad things like we used to be.

Despite what you may have been taught or heard preached or were told, there really are only four levels of existence to go.

Oblivion, when you screw up the other three and cease to be.

Living, which we aren't anymore.

Heaven, where only the good people go.

And Hell, where the rest of us went. But Hell had many levels. Kinda like a country club or a luxury cruise ship. The higher price you were worth, the closer you got to the better buffet line.

So Bounce, who some say lost everyone he ever

loved to something so evil it spawned an army, gave you an option to stay in the world of the living as long as you obeyed the rules.

He called us Breakers. I was never sure if Bounce was a Breaker, but he never really sat down to reminisce. Breakers were immortal badasses who had done horrible things against mankind or had a made a bad choice that caused an innocent person in their human lives to lose their life. At the split second the gates of Hell were opening up to welcome you to the frying pan, Bounce was there to pay a coin to keep you from burning. The purpose of Breakers was to eliminate the Energy Eaters who preyed upon mankind and the energy of their life essences—the very energy that attached a human's soul to their body.

It paid well and had a ton of fringe benefits. Sounds awesome, doesn't it?

Yeah, shame no one asked me. I never wanted it. I never needed it. I was actually, for the few minutes my brain worked before we died, happy to be dying. It would be over, and I wouldn't be contained and controlled by another person. Now, Jess *and* Bounce controlled me. No one knew his real name, but his nickname was acquired because if you weren't going by the rules, your new immortality would be bounced back into the dead, no more second chance zone.

That sounded nice to me.

So my new goal was to get that bounce. To make it end. We had spent one hundred and fifty years since we were killed doing the fucking greater good. And Jess was now more gifted than ever. You think he was deadly before? He was even more so now. And now he had the approval to be so from the powers that be.

But what was causing me the most pain? His brain. He had now gotten so good at keeping me in my place that I only came out when he was in absolute agony, and he couldn't deal. Whereas we were friends once and then tolerated each other while he was human, we were now enemies. I wanted him dead, and he wanted me gone. I was his deep, dark secret that he was terrified someone would find out about.

What would people think of a flawed hero? That had a nagging deadly voice in his head? Yeah, greater good would probably view that as less than a heroic icon. And Jess just loved being a hero.

And he was good at it, too. Respect, honor, trust, and worship—all the things he didn't have as a human. And none of the things I could or would ever have. Kind of impossible if no one knew you existed.

So I spent my time numb and nonexistent or bored out of my fucking mind. One hundred and fifty years of boredom.

Of only getting the bad.

And never, ever getting the good. Something had to give.

And then it did.

Enter Witch.

C H A P T E R   E L E V E N

Time-out

What do you mean? Time-out?
Jess was packing and not very happy about it. "Easy, you fucked up. An innocent was hurt. So we've been ordered to take a time-out." A shirt got wadded up and tossed in the duffel. "On some damn island."

An island? Wow. Just like almost all of the cool immortal heroes, the sun was not our friend. To go after the bogeyman that lurked in the dark, you had to be one with the dark. So the sun was like a microwave to a hamster. Bad.

I guess saying I'm sorry doesn't help?

Jess' movements stopped, but the smirk on his face grew. I couldn't see it, but boy, oh boy, could I feel it. He had that smirk down pat. The packing started up again, and then the bag was zipped up.

When are we leaving?

Jess slung the strap onto his shoulder, tugged on his Stetson, and grumbled, "Now."

Ever been to a tropical island? Probably not, huh. It's bright and hot, and I was not happy. Not to mention, if Jess were in time-out, I would be in—all the time. There was no fighting here, no violence, no bloodshed, so no need for me to be out. I hated being in. It had made me claustrophobic and—okay, don't laugh—scared of the dark.

Real badass right?

We had been there for two days, Jess

grumbling in the main house while I sat in the dark and cold of the hole. I was miserable but gave up whining and complaining after being locked down and in on day one. I was sitting there, getting angrier by the second about, well, everything, when I heard that voice again. I hadn't heard it for a long time. My head snapped up, and I tried to focus on the darkness, but the cold wind that always blew made it hard.

Until it came again.

I can help you. Get out. Have control.

I pushed to my feet, and cocking my head, I listened for which direction it was coming from. But it seemed to come from everywhere. And nowhere. "Who's there?"

Do you want my help? Yes or no. Answer quick.

Before I could even give it any thought—remember that thing about bad decisions? Yeah, this is one of those times—I said, "Yes! Yes. Help me. Let me out. Please?"

Then.

I was.

C H A P T E R   T W E L V E

Just one night

I had no idea who or what allowed me out, but I was not wasting time. I paced that small space as the sun was out. A maid came by, and I growled and threw a book at her head, luckily missing. I didn't mean to, but all I wanted was for that damn sun to set. Throwing open the door, I looked left then right down the hall.

Since Jess had me locked away, I had no idea what this place was like. He was so pissed we were there that he didn't allow me to see what he saw. Running down the hall, I went down the stairs, going low to see if anyone else was in the big, fancy house. No, it seemed empty.

The sun was setting fast, and I made a beeline for the door until I heard that voice.

"Hey. I made some sandwiches."

My hand paused on the doorknob, and I glanced over my shoulder, and that was when I saw her. Witch.

Beautiful dark hair, gorgeous green eyes, and a smile that made you believe in God. Any god, didn't matter which one. She turned and beckoned for me to follow, and my eyes snapped to the knob, but my hand slid off it to turn and go after her. Sucker.

I didn't know why, and I would curse myself dozens of times for not running and count myself a lucky ass that I hadn't, too. But that's for later. For now? I just wanted to know her more.

She stood in the very spacious kitchen making—like she said—sandwiches.

I peeked in, and she looked up.

"Hey, Jess. I made enough for you. Figured you'd be getting hungry."

Oh, right, Jess. No one other than Bounce knew about me. Walking in, I shoved my hands in my pockets and leaned against the counter. "Uh. Thank you."

She narrowed her eyes as if she were on to me and then held out the plate. "Roast beef and Swiss cheese work?"

I nodded and took one, eyes going down to look at her long fingers and noticed no ring. Oh, well, that made it even better. I flashed a smile and stopped myself just short of showing fangs. I wasn't sure if she knew what we were or not.

She gave an amused smile. "It's okay. Don't you remember?" She pointed to herself. "Me, healer. You, Breaker."

Oh, good. She did know. My smile grew, and I bit into the sandwich. "Guess I forgot."

She nodded and sat down at a table and chairs, and I walked over and sat down, too. I was getting crumbs all over the table and raised a brow as she stood and grabbed a paper towel. "Forgot your manners, too?"

I looked up and then back down at the crumbs. "Uh. Sorry."

She smiled again and leaned over to clean up the crumbs.

Her hair was right in front of me, and I couldn't resist, so I leaned closer and breathed it in. Oh, wow. It smelled like vanilla and lavender. I closed my eyes, soaking it in, loving the way it made me think of flowers in the dark.

"Uh, Jess?"

My eyes snapped open to find her looking at me. A smile, nervous and hesitant, tilted my lips.

"Hi."

She laughed and sat back down. "You're acting kind of odd. I know we just met two days ago, but you're acting, different. More"—she crinkled her nose in the cutest way—"odd."

I stiffened and sat up straight. "Sorry. I'm, uh, just having an off morning, I guess."

I did an internal check right then to see if Jess was beating down the walls of our brain to get out. And got nothing but total silence in return, which was not the norm. I did, however, get a moment they had shared. She was here for losing control of her magic because she was not only a healer but also a witch. She had been put in time-out just like Jess had been. Handy info. Not much, but it was at least something. But I needed to snap into acting like Jess, or this beautiful woman was going to be onto me.

My eyes slid to the windows and saw that the sun had set. All I wanted to do was to go outside. I had never seen an ocean or a beach.

Or an island.

In fact, the total sum of my experiences had been scenes of fights, washes of blood, and seedy death scenes.

The thought of a beach at night, on my own, had my mouth watering.

Shoving the sandwich into my mouth, I chewed, trying to swallow it down. I had no idea how much time I had, so I stood, gave her a nod, and headed for the hall to make the most of it.

I didn't even realize the woman had followed. I

was too caught up in digging my feet into the sand, laughing at how it felt. I was looking at the strange moon, the dark sky, and the waves that seemed to glow when they crashed to the shore. It was so beautiful. Now, keep in mind that I don't get a lot of beautiful.

But tonight? I felt like I had hit the jackpot the moment that woman stepped in front of me.

"You okay?"

I looked down at her and smiled. "It's beautiful, isn't it?"

She laughed and looked around us. "Yeah. But you weren't very impressed yesterday. Actually, you seemed kind of pissed."

I frowned at that. "Was I?"

Jess must have taken this all for granted, but I could never take anything for granted. It was always taken away before I could get jaded by it, I guess.

The woman nodded, and I realized I had no idea who she was and didn't even know her name. Jess probably knew, but I didn't have a clue beyond the moment I came across. Okay, so I knew she was a witch, so I decided right then and there, her name would be Witch.

"Want to walk with me?"

I looked down at her when she asked that question. A walk? With her? Here? Oh yes. Please. Please.

She held out her hand, and I looked at it like it was totally strange to me. Because it really was. She smiled at me, and I couldn't help but smile back as I took her hand.

As we walked, she let me know that she too had let her powers go out of whack, and Bounce had offered her refuge here to calm down as it seemed powers didn't work on this island. I found it hard to believe this woman would hurt anyone. She was so gentle and sweet.

As we walked, I soaked up the sensation of her hand in mine. It was so soft and warm that I got lost in it, so much so I didn't realize we were walking so close together that our arms pressed against each other's sides. Her voice was like a lullaby and made me so calm. I was never calm, never at peace, yet her voice put me there. That, too, was new. And I didn't just like it, I loved it.

She told me about her family and her sisters and everything. I found out her name was Emma Devenmore, and she had two sisters and one brother, who they had lost when she was a kid. She told me all these things like I was a good guy. Then again, she thought I was Jess, but that was okay. It was worth it. Something about her made me feel like I had never felt before.

Whole. Complete. Good.

We walked and talked for hours. When Witch asked about my past, I had to use Jess's since I really didn't have one of my own, well, one that was suitable to tell her. My own memories were brutal, violent, and deadly. But Jess had some nice ones since he got to live the good parts of our life.

The moon rose, and it seemed like the sand glowed under the silvery light. She fell quiet, and I turned to look at her. "What's wrong?"

She shrugged, and I tilted my head to try to catch her gaze.

"You can tell me. I'm good at keeping secrets." I was. After all, I was one of the biggest secrets that existed.

Emma looked up at me and said softly, "I was wondering if you would kiss me."

I blinked at that, and before I could stop it, her hand pulled away from mine as if rejected. I had never kissed a *woman* before. That one kiss with Heaven had been both my first and my last.

I was always afraid to share that kind of intimacy, afraid I would be made to pay the price, or worse, the one I kissed would pay the same price as Heaven.

My eyes drifted left, then right, unsure of what to do next.

Witch laughed softly, but it was a pained sound, not funny but sad. "Forget I said anything. I just have never felt so sure about someone before."

My eyes went back to hers and then dropped to her mouth. Her lips were sun-kissed and pink, and I wondered if they tasted of vanilla like the smell of her skin. "Sure?" My voice cracked, and I couldn't help but step closer, eyes fixated on her sweet-looking mouth, hoping she would speak again just so that I could watch it move.

She gave me a nervous smile. "You're just so easy to talk to. And so, well, you're different than you were before. Sweeter now. Not as sure. It's cute."

I rolled my eyes and went to pull away. "Oh, well. Uh. Thanks?"

She laughed, and this time, it was her that kept my hand in hers. "It's not that. You're just night and day than what you weretwo days ago."

She stepped up closer and placed her hand on my chest. That sent my heart racing like a drum as if the drummer was playing it really, really fast.

Meeting her gaze, I swallowed hard and said, my voice still unsure, "I guess I needed some rest or something." I smiled. "Or really good sandwiches."

Witch laughed that musical laugh, and then it

faded as she stepped right up to me. I blinked, swallowed again, and before I knew it, she was on her tiptoes in the sand and was pressing those lips I had been fascinated with all night against mine.

It tingled and was so warm, and it scared the absolute crap out of me. But then her arms came up to wrap around my neck, fingers playing in my hair, and it felt so nice. My arms came around her, and I kissed her back. I had no idea what to do, but as her lips softened against mine, I went on instinct. My tongue came out to tease, and I was full of surprise when her tongue greeted mine.

We kissed deep and gentle, but it became so much more. Soon, I was totally getting into this kissing thing. I felt Witch's heart racing against my chest, her soft breasts pressing against me. My hands moved down her back, splaying my fingers against the small of it, wanting her closer, nearer. Wanting so much more and yet so grateful if this was all I got.

It wasn't long before our kiss became so heated and demanding that we were both breathless. Witch broke first and whispered against my lips, "You are such a good kisser. I had no idea."

I smiled and whispered back, "Neither did I."

She laughed, and we kissed again. I felt things I had never felt before—happiness, thrilled, hot, and melted on the inside and cooled by her touch on the outside. And completely and totally aroused. I shifted my hips, trying not to embarrass or scare her by just how much, and my hardness pressed against her stomach.

We ended that kiss, and she met my eyes. "Spend the night with me, Jess."

My brain, well, *our* brain ignored the name she called me. A reminder that I wasn't who she thought I was. But she seemed to like me more, which she said so herself. And it appeared she had never kissed Jess. I frowned for a minute, feeling unsure if this was wrong. Or right.

But maybe wrong was right since all I was allowed to have, or do, or keep were the wrong things. "Yes. Please."

She took my hand and led me back to the house. We didn't talk, and I kept waiting for Jess to jump out, take control, and ruin this all. Or even worse, take it for himself just like he had done so many times before with so much of the good in our existence. But as we walked into the house, she came back to me to kiss again, and this time, the need made me hurt in all the good ways. Ways I had never even dared.

Before I knew it, we were in her room. The linen curtains on the opened windows billowed in the night breeze, the moon making the room glow as she backed away from me. I whimpered thinking she changed her mind, but I was wrong as she pulled her T-shirt over her head and stepped out of her shorts. I had seen nude women before but always from the inside of Jess's head. And they were never getting undressed for me. Always Jess.

"You're so beautiful, Witch."

I had never seen someone so beautiful, so breathtaking, and knowing she was going to be mine, one night or not, almost made me more scared than anything else. She held out her hand, and I took it, stepping close to her again and breathing in the scent of her sun-kissed skin, the vanilla scent even stronger now.

Taking both of her hands in mine, I looked down at her, and I was so nervous, my hands shook as they tightened around hers. "Are you sure? I mean, I don't—I've never." I stopped myself. Jess was known as a womanizer, and to say we had never been with a woman wouldn't make any sense.

Because of that, I was a total virgin, a fact that was getting in the way. She would know. She would guess, and then things would go really bad. She would stop, kick me out, and call me a monster if she figured it out. And that was the scariest thing ever.

Witch pulled my head down to kiss me again, and that calmed me—weird, but it was instant as if she chased all the fear and confusion away with the simple touch of her kiss. I brought my hands up to cup her face as she led me back toward the bed. She helped me off with my shirt, and all I wanted to do was kiss her again. Her fingers grazed over all the scars, all the marks of battles fought and won, and I kissed her again. I was getting drunk on her kiss and was so overwhelmed in the sensation that it wasn't until her fingers brushed my hardness that I realized she had undone my jeans, and they were now around my ankles. I stiffened all over at that and swallowed as I met her eyes.

She gave me the sweetest smile as her hand stroked me, and it felt incredible. My eyes drifted closed, and then I was falling, landing on something soft and scented. Scented like her.

She straddled me on the bed and put the sweetest kisses on my chest, pausing to tease my nipples, which made me snort and her laugh. It tickled, I couldn't help it. She looked down at me as I glanced up, afraid I had done something wrong, but all I saw was kindness, and wow, she was aroused… by me.

That changed something deep inside, and without thought, I rolled her over and covered her body with mine, claiming her mouth again.

Sweet and tender was replaced with raw desire and need. My hands wanted to touch everywhere, so they did. My lips wanted to taste everything, so I did. I did that for a long while, loving the sounds she made and the way her body writhed and twisted so I could taste more of her. She was so moist and hot and tasted like vanilla—liquid and sweet. She wrapped her legs around my shoulders and dug her heels into my back. I must have been doing it right because before I knew it, she was crying out, her body arching and thrusting against my mouth. I liked that, the sensation and the power of knowing I did that. I made her moan, and I made her have so much pleasure. Me.

I was going to do it more, but she dug her fingers into my hair and tugged, her nails biting deliciously at my scalp as she said with a gasp, "Please. I want you."

I crawled up her body on my hands and knees, kissing a trail up and nipping at her soft skin with my fangs, and when I reached her mouth, I kissed her deep and slow, letting her taste how sweet she was mixed with me. Then, like finding my way home without knowing the way, I was inside, and I froze, not moving. The feeling was like nothing I had ever felt.

She was so warm and tight, perfect in every way. I blinked as I held myself up on my forearms, looking down at her beautiful face, flushed with passion, lips full from my kisses. And I knew that something was happening. Something was changing inside of me, and there was no going back. I felt something I had never felt before, something I was never designed to feel and was as forbidden as an apple in that garden in the Bible. I just had no idea what it was.

Her eyes opened, dark green with desire, and she frowned. "Jess?"

My eyes snapped to hers, and with a deep voice, hoarse with emotions I didn't understand swirling in my head, sparking places never meant to be lit up, I whispered, "Don't. Don't say that name."

She went to ask what I meant, but I brought my mouth down to hers, kissing her as my hips started to move. It felt like heaven and earth. Hell and damnation, and I wanted it all. I didn't care about the consequences, nor did I care about tomorrow. I just wanted her in every way, and not just physically, not just her body, as we were joined now. No, I wanted all of her. And it was so wrong.

She started moaning and thrashing beneath me, her hips coming up to meet my every thrust, surrounding me in wet velvet heat, clenching around me and driving me toward an edge I wanted to reach with her, a cliff I wanted to fall off, holding her close so no one could find us. To keep her in the dark, a dark I always lived. She'd be my light, and I would burn with the happiness of it.

My groans joined hers as our bodies moved in a dance that I knew I was never meant to learn, steps I wasn't allowed to take. Soon, we were slick with sweat, our thrusts and plunges frantic and urgent as the power of our desire overtook us.

I didn't want it to end. I begged for it not to in my head. But she felt so perfect, and I had never felt this before. Soon, she was screaming and started to say that name again, but I brought my hand up to cover her mouth, that name like acid to the emotions I was still trying to figure out. She arched up as if she liked that, and I tensed, threw my head back, and roared out in my release deep inside, her clenching heat all around me. She brought my head down to kiss me, breathless and panting as I kept moving my hips, not wanting to miss a single second of her climax, not sure if mine would ever end.

But it did, and then it was over. As I lay on my back, she curled up against my side, making lazy circles on my sweat-slick chest with her fingers, and whispered, "What were you going to say before? You didn't what?"

I looked over at her and opened my mouth then closed it. How could I tell her I didn't know what to do? It seemed silly now considering I seemed to have figured it out as we went along. I smiled. "I don't even remember. Must not have been important."

She laughed softly and kissed the spot over my heart. God, how I wished that were my heart. For the first time ever, it was the only part I wished I really had. Just for her. But I wouldn't have it long because it would be hers. I had no doubt in the world about that.

The breeze coming in the windows was welcome, cooling our skin. She rested an arm on my chest and put her chin on it then looked up at me.

"Do you want to barbecue tomorrow? You said you were really good at barbecuing. And omelets."

I did? No, wait, Jess must have said that.

She smiled, and I frowned, looking away.

Tomorrow? How did I know if I would even be here tomorrow?

Bringing my gaze back to hers, I searched her beautiful evergreen depths for a sign that she knew, trust being a new thing to me, as well. But all I saw was total adoration and concern—and something else. But my brain didn't register that any more than it registered that she thought she'd had sex with and now laying beside a man I wasn't.

"Sure. I'd like that." She smiled and laid her head down.

My eyes went to the window and stared at the moon. "Emma?"

She looked back up and said softly, "Yeah?"

I cupped her face and brought it down to mine. "Can we do that again?"

And we did.

Three times.

And then morning came.

The only bad and sad thing about that was...

She wanted omelets. Jess made omelets. I never could. She got her omelet.

And I was back in the dark.

CHAPTER THIRTEEN

Pay-per-view, not

It was months.

Long, torturous months that Jess put me away alone in the dark and the cold. But he changed the terms of my imprisonment.

See, after that day, that one wonderful night, Jess and Emma got together. He used the night I gave her to start a relationship. You know, one of those bittersweet love stories you read about in those cheesy novels? Yeah. That.

While that was painful enough, it wasn't the worst of it. No, the worst part was he punished me for being with her, for coming out and taking control—something I still didn't know how I did—by teaching the most painful lesson possible in the most painful way he could.

I got to see and hear everything. Everything that mattered.

So as I sat in the hole, in the dark and cold, it would suddenly all play out like a projection on the walls in full color and sound for me to be tortured by.

So unlike the century before, when I would go into a numb and unknowing stasis for months, I was made to watch the woman I loved, the only woman I had ever been with, fall in love with a man I was learning to hate with a murderous vengeance.

I had to see every laugh and smile from her to him. See every kiss, hug, and touch. And even worse than that?

I had to watch them make love. I closed my eyes every time and wrapped my arms around my head, rocking and screaming to please make it stop. But the sounds I could always hear. Her crying out his name, her moans, and his, all of it—sound and picture—in stereo because I had no escape; there was nowhere to go.

My torture took its toll. If Jess was teaching me a lesson that he would make me hurt if I took something from him, I learned it. That created a new goal for me—make him hurt as much as he was hurting me.

So when I did get to drive, I made it as painful and as violent as possible. I wanted him dead and didn't care if that meant I died, too. We were stabbed, beaten, bloodied, and got gutted a few times.

But even that came back at me for whom did he go to for healing, care, and tenderness? My. Witch.

I got to see that, too.

Every time I was out, once the obsessive need to hurt him faded, I would think to go to Witch and explain it all to her. But with the wane of that need came a calm, and I would be right back inside. He had gotten very good at keeping me leashed.

And I hated him even more for that.

So as those months went by, I hated him more and more. And he hated me. It was at least mutual. The only bright spots—those times when they would eat dinner, share lunch, or watch a movie—were also the most painful spots. I saw it all from his eyes, and sometimes, I would trick myself into thinking it was me she was talking to, who she smiled at and touched.

Until she said his name and then the fantasy would crumble, and the reality would tear me apart.

I would scream, beg, and plead for Jess to

please just put me back in the nothing so I wouldn't know what was happening. His response was total silence, but the torture, the punishment continued.

And I was going insane. Well, more insane than I was before.

I paced then just sat for the longest of times, hoping to send myself into oblivion as I wrapped my arms around my head and sang at the top of my lungs so as not to hear nor see. But nothing stopped the agony.

I could neither watch nor look away.

Because that was the only way I could see her. So it was agony and bliss, and pain and pleasure, which would become a trend. And not one that I ever wanted to set. But destiny and fate were not always friends. In my case?

They downright hated each other.

Eventually, it dulled as I surrendered to my punishment.

Jess and Emma had been together for four months, and part of me didn't understand how that was possible. The night Witch and I spent together was just so special to me that I didn't see how she could be with him. Until I had to remind myself that to her, it was a night with him.

I didn't exist. I was no one that she knew or would ever know. It was how it was designed, how I was made. But something had changed inside of me. I started craving and wanting as I had never done before for something so forbidden and unthought of for over a century, simply because I had not dared to do so.

A life. Of my own.

Or death.

To us both.

CHAPTER FOURTEEN

I'm the one

I thought about the best way to make death happen because, well, let's be honest here, if all you were was a voice in someone's head, the chances of you getting your own flesh high-rise were pretty slim. Not to mention, I didn't see any way Jess would even allow that. He was too used to being in control and using me for the bad things, dealing with the pain and the violence, all coated in layers of blood for the good of man.

So how do you take down a hero who is the one in control as well as your host, who you hate as much as any of the enemies in a comic book or movie?

Easy.

You just stop.

Now Jess had to deal with all the bad and the violence, the pain and the fear, as I simply refused to handle it whenever I felt the draw calling me out. See, that whole torturing me for so long, using his gifts to do so, gave me a chance to hone some of my own, and I had gotten just as good.

Ignoring and resisting.

Handy, huh? Yeah, I thought so, too.

So time went on, and I had to admit, I took great joy in seeing him get more and more out of control. He and Emma often fought, heated and terrible fights while I sat there in our headspace, laughing and cheering her on. God, she was beautiful when she was mad.

Jess? When he was mad? Yeah, no, not so much. In fact, it was pretty ugly.

"What the hell, Sundown?" Jess had been out on patrol, chasing down bad things, and it had not gone well. Now he sat there, digging two slugs out of our shoulder and had been trying to get me to respond, at least in the aftermath, for about an hour.

I sat with my back turned to his eyes' view, my arms wrapped around my knees, and my forehead pressed on them when I glanced back over my shoulder.

What do you mean, Jess? Crap, I had not meant to answer. But well, I had gotten so used to us having conversations that it came naturally to answer. I'd have to work on that for this to end up as I wanted.

"Oh, now you talk?"

He stopped digging out the bullets, dark red blood running down his arm, and said in a low voice, "I know you're pissed. And I know why you're pissed. But if you keep this avoiding your purpose shit, we'll both be dead. Now"—he commenced prodding around in the bullet holes in our shoulder again—"you don't want that, now do you?"

Actually, that was what I wanted. I opened my mouth to answer then closed it and just wrapped my arms tighter around my knees, gritted my teeth, and focused on not answering back.

"Jess? You okay?"

Witch. My head snapped up, and I got to my feet, turning around to see her through Jess's eyes. She looked tired, and her face was drawn from stress. They had argued again, and it was mostly my fault. She wanted him to stay home and completely heal since he was getting hurt worse, and more damage was done each time he returned. That was my fault. I was the one with the skills when it got so bad. I was the ruthless, deadly one, not him.

I don't know why I didn't think about the effect all of this would have on Witch. Would she be hurt and sad when we died?

Oh, I was pretty sure she would be. She loved Jess because that was the kind of person Witch was. She was perfect, sweet, and cared about everyone. But their relationship was not meant to be, and they both knew it. It was the core of what was wrong with it. He knew she wasn't the "one"—yeah, that whole romance ideology. Lame, I know—and she just really wanted to be the one.

If she only knew whose one she was, but a lot of good that did me—nada, zilch, zero, zippo.

She walked over and knelt to see his wounds, and I sighed as her fingers touched him. I felt those soft, caring caresses, and I closed my eyes to enjoy the moment more, hating myself for doing so. Good thing I didn't have morals, or I would feel like a sleazy Peeping Tom all this time.

She didn't know she was touching me. She just thought she was touching Jess, but even like this, she soothed and calmed me, made me feel how I felt that one time with her.

Known.

Jess shook his head but let her dress his wounds and get the bullets out. "It's fine, darling. I'll heal."

His gaze met hers, and I stepped forward as he looked deep into her eyes. I was always looking to see if there was any sign she had finally realized that the man she had spent that night with four months ago was not the man that was before her now.

I was disappointed every time.

"You can't keep doing this." Her eyes went down to the task, wiping the blood away and bandaging the wounds.

I went down to my haunches to try to get a whiff of her dark hair, of the vanilla scent she always smelled so sweet of. I got disappointed about that every time too. Jess's head was not smell-a-vision, just sight-and-sound-a-view.

"Emma. It's my job. You know that. I have to do it. You knew that when we met." He stood up and tossed his bloody, shot up shirt before grabbing another and sliding it on.

Emma got up and stood there, wrapping her arms around herself.

"I know, Jess. But"—her voice took on an odd quality, and there was an even weirder look on her face—"there's something I have to tell you."

Jess turned to face her. "What is it, Ems?"

He walked up and gently put his hands on her arms, full of concern.

She started crying, and as he pulled her into our arms, I longed to feel her tears. I bet they were so warm. Not like I ever wanted to cause her to cry, never, but to be there for her? Feeling that warm, salty sensation soaking into my skin? Oh, yeah, I would have loved that.

Jess started kissing her tears away, and I was turning away so I didn't have to see when she said something. I turned back, a puzzled look on my face as I tried to figure out what she said, but suddenly, everything went black.

"Jess? Hey! What happened?"

And like that, the torture of my seeing them together ended. I mourned it. I mourned her. And that was the beginning of the end.

CHAPTER FIFTEEN

Broke her heart?

If I thought I was going insane before seeing Jess and Witch together, I was kidding myself. Jess was smart. Real smart. Always had been, and now, I was a glutton to be punished like before. At least then I could see Witch even if it was indirectly.

So I came back out and hated myself for being so weak, but he still didn't give me glimpses. I didn't understand it. I couldn't seem to do right, and doing wrong wasn't getting me anywhere, either. Jess had become sullen, and if he was cranky before, he was ten times crankier now. He snarled and growled, cursed and ranted. He had these internal dialogues with himself, but those, too, were now blocked from me. They had never been blocked before, which was how I knew what was going on.

But one night, when I was trying to prove to Jess that I was going to do my part, my job if he would let me have my front-row seat back, I got an unexpected and unplanned gift.

It just took a lot of blood, a lot of pain, and my total and complete resolve.

It was a rainy night in San Francisco, which wasn't that strange since it rained here a lot—*a lot* a lot. Jess had been on patrol and got ambushed. He fought long and hard but took some heavy damage. As he felt himself weaken, I waited in the wings, bouncing on my feet, ready to be out until like that, as it was in the past, I was.

I spun, kicked, and punched, blood flying and was laughing in the joy of it all. The demons we fought—which, if you didn't know better, looked just like humans. They put off this vibe that if you were immortal and trained to do so, you could pick up on. They fed off humans, and blood, sex, and agony were their feasts.

They were mostly cowards and chose the weak and frail, women, and even children. The only way they could keep up their human form was to devour the essence of humans. If they didn't keep their human form, they were not able to survive here, and their home in Hell, well, it wasn't near as fun. So they used humans to be humans. It wasn't done in a painless or nice manner. Not one bit. The more violent the death, the higher the endorphins in the human and the stronger their level of adrenaline, the more intoxicating their essences were to the demons, which meant they could hold their human form for longer.

They were mistaken for all kinds of things, none of which were right—bloodsuckers, vampires, fangers. I knew those things existed because I had met a few, but we focused on Energy Eaters, which was what they were.

Oh, anyway, back to what I was doing. What was that again? Oh, yeah.

One ran at me, and I went low, tossing it over my back, and spun to slice through its throat. The foulest blood sprayed me. It smelled a bit like an old dumpster combined with as many smelly, disgusting things as you could find, all brewed together in a stew. It tasted even worse if you could even imagine anything worse than that. I probably could, but I'm kinda not right in the head.

I was happily spraying the Eaters' life juice all over the place when I realized I had killed them all. Dang it!

That meant playtime was over, and I would be going back.

I dropped down to sit, my legs feeling like rubber, and wiped the blood from my eyes and face as it was sticky in my hair and starting to cake and crack.

The healing would start taking place in a few minutes, and that would trigger Jess to come back up. The Eaters were all dissolving into this roadkill-looking sludge since their true forms couldn't exist here and death destroyed the essences they had consumed. It smelled terrible, too. But it seemed fitting when you thought about how gross they were and what they did.

Pain keeps him away. Use it.

As my head snapped up, I narrowed my eyes and looked around. "Hello?"

But the Eater sludge wasn't able to talk, well, mostly because they were dissolving and goo didn't have mouths. And I had heard that voice before. It was the same one that had given me the chance to be with Witch that one night.

"So where the heck have you been?" I asked as I got to my feet, flicking sludge off my fingers. God, it would be nice if they turned into fairy dust or something because Eater sludge was gross. Like some kind of demon snot or something. "And while you're all talkative, who the heck are you?"

I found some sludge in my ear and grimaced. "Because between you and me? It's like really crowded in the head now. Two is plenty."

Pain keeps him away.

I raised a brow and nodded. "Yeah, you kinda

said that before. But that didn't answer my questions."
I waited and got silence. That was weird.

I heard the sounds of sirens in the distance and scooped up my dagger off the ground, and that was when it made sense as the light from the streetlight glimmered off the bloodied edge.

"Pain keeps him away!" I smiled and laughed. "Oh, wow! I totally get it. Thank you."

I took off at a lope, away from the scene of the crime, and lifted the sleeve of my jacket to expose my arm underneath it. Ducking into an alley as the red and blues passed me going the other way, I could already feel that weird disconnected feeling I got when I was being put away.

Lifting the blade to my arm, I sliced, letting out a hiss as a trickle of crimson welled up then dripped to the pavement.

It was like being plugged back in lightning sharp from the disconnect. I looked at the wound and laughed again. Bringing the knife up, I licked the blade before sheathing it. I had one goal in mind, one place to go, and it was located by the bay.

Witch's house.

CHAPTER SIXTEEN

Point A to point B

San Francisco is full of hills. Lots and lots of hills. Have you ever run up a hill? It's hard, especially when you're already weak, bleeding, and making stops to bleed some more on purpose.

Jess and the others can blur. What's blur, you ask? Why, I'll tell you. This is how Bounce tells it, so, uh, keep it between us. He is not my biggest fan, but more about why that is later.

Okay, so imagine drawing a point A on one side of the city and a point B on the other side. Now, draw a line between the two of them. Normal people—mortal humans—and probably a lot of other things have to walk that line from point A to point B, right?

Well, we don't. We call it blur because we literally blur and smudge that line in our head and *poof*, we are at point B with point A being way over there. So, see? Blur.

But here's the thing. I suck at blurring. I've tried and tried, and every time, I end up not where I want to be. One time, I tried to blur away from danger and, instead, ended up in more danger. But uh, naked. Yeah, that is a story that will never be told, so don't even try. Not even for the best candy ever.

So, there I was running across the city to get to Witch's house and getting odd looks, even though it was three in the morning. San Fran has a pretty active club scene, but most of the people vacating the dens of fun and hook-ups were both drunk and stoned or a combo of some other substances that dulled the senses. So that was a benefit to me.

It took me until almost four in the morning to get to Witch's brownstone by the bay. It was a renovated older home with her shop for herbals and holistic tonics on the bottom floor and her living on the top two floors. There were no lights on, and I paced along her porch, slicing into my arm once again to let the pain give me more time.

I thought maybe I should knock or ring the bell or something. But then I realized and pulled Jess's keys out. Ha! Of course, he had a key and using it, I opened her front door quietly, being careful to close it silently behind me. The shop was full of so many herbs, plants, and oils, and it smelled really good. The hardwood floor gleamed in the moonlight coming from the windows, casting shadows against the crown molding, and the dark shelves that held numerous jars of ancient remedies for just about everything and gave the place a musty, earthy smell. But then underneath that was the subtle scent of vanilla, and I smiled.

My Witch.

Going to the stairs, I climbed up to the very top floor quietly, glancing into the homey living area and modern kitchen, which gleamed with stainless steel, then climbed up to where the master bedroom loft was. It had windows that you could see the bay from, and moonlight lit up the room.

At first, I didn't think she was there, but then she rolled, murmuring in her sleep, and that was when I lost my breath. God, she was so beautiful as her hair spread over the pillow, dark as midnight against the silver of the moonlit sheets.

Walking over, I crouched down and just stared

at her sleeping, wanting to touch her so badly, but afraid that if I did, I would wake her or scare her. I never wanted to scare her. Or make her cry.

So I stayed there, content with just breathing in the same air as she was. Her exhale became my inhale as I closed my eyes, and that sweet, sensual scent of vanilla made me sway, causing me to put a hand out to stop myself on the bed.

"Jess?"

My eyes snapped open to meet her half-open green ones, sleep softening her voice. I couldn't move as I looked at her. My mouth opened to speak, and I was speechless. She sat up level with me, and she saw the blood and gore.

"You're hurt again. Oh, Jess."

Her gaze moved down to my arm, and then she saw the blade in my hand, which rested on the bed. Her face was awash with confusion as she got up and out of bed instantly. Now I was confused.

"Wait. Let me explain." I put up both my hands, and she shoved me, hard.

"No! You break my damn heart, tell me you don't love me, and then you show up here like that? With a knife? You think you can use me like a freaking ER?" She grabbed a bottle off her dresser and threw it.

I dodged it easily, but my brain was sputtering and missing sparks like crazy. Broke her heart? Didn't love her? What? I blinked at her for what seemed like hours but was only seconds. She was crying, and I had no idea what to do. "Don't love you? What?"

She shook her head, covering her face with her hands. "I can't do this. You can't take back what you said. I don't know why you're here, but go." She dropped her hands. "Please. Get out!" She put out her hand. "And give me my key. Now."

I just stared in confusion and moved as if made out of Play-Doh, reaching into my pocket then handing her the key. "What did I say? I don't understand. Wait, no!"

I had forgotten... she thought I was Jess. Maybe this was my chance. Maybe I could explain, fix whatever it was that Jess had done. But she was so hurt, screaming and crying, and I had no idea how to deal with it. I had no skills, no abilities to handle it. This was definitely bad but not any type of bad I'd ever had to deal with before.

"Get out! Now! Go! It was so easy for you before! Do it again!"

She shoved me again toward her bedroom door, and I tried to stop her by reaching out to take her arm. She just got that much more upset and screamed louder. It was too much, and I didn't want her more upset, crying more. Not because of me, never because of me.

I stumbled down the stairs and out the door and started running toward the bay.

The water was covered in fog, obscuring the Golden Gate Bridge like some dinosaur rising out of the mist. "What did you do? Jess! What did you do! You hurt her!"

What I had to do.

And then my time-out was over.

CHAPTER SEVENTEEN

I don't want the bad, not anymore.

You don't hurt my Witch.

Let's get this straight, here and now—past, present, or future. Okay, so you guys don't know the future, but I do, and you will, too—just not yet.

You don't hurt my Witch.

Hurt me, stab me, be cruel to me, but you never ever hurt my Witch.

Jess had not only hurt my Witch but he had also broken her heart. She said so herself. And that, to me, was unforgivable. Punishable by death, no reprieve, no probation, or governor pardon. And I had ranted, seethed, and bellowed it inside Jess's head. I demanded to know what he had done and why he had broken her heart. What wasn't I seeing? I got no answers or response. The rift between us was too wide, too deep, and not able to heal. It was overflowing to the brink with nothing but resentment and hate.

Jess knew that if he let me out, he was doomed. I would provide the killing blow myself if I had to, not even thinking about how one beheads themselves. I would have found a way—lay on the trolley tracks, step in front of a truck—I would have figured out a way to make it end, to get revenge and make it where he could never hurt Witch again.

So I was locked up tight and put away. Cold and dark, not able to see anything of what was happening beyond in the life I was never able to have except in bits and pieces of pain and suffering. My suffering was made worse with my memories, my own thoughts. My mind—well, what I guess was the part of Jess's that was mine—went from the night spent with Witch to the last night I had seen her.

Her screaming so hurt and upset, shoving me and telling me to go. I had to force myself to believe she was telling Jess to go, not me. She didn't know about me. But there was a part that thought maybe she did. Maybe he had told her, and when she realized it was me rather than Jess there, she didn't want me.

She wanted him.

That was the most gut check thought of all. I became more and more lost in my sorrow and depression that I had no idea the toll this was taking on Jess. I found out when Bounce showed up in the most unlikely of places. Who knew Jess's head had a welcome mat?

"What exactly is your plan?"

I was sitting on the floor of the hole—which was what I called the dark, cold, windy small space Jess kept me locked away in—when I heard Bounce's voice… No way. But when I looked up and saw the tall being standing there, it was a total what-the-fuck moment.

I got to my feet fast and scrambled against the wall, pressing my back against it as I blinked, wondering if Bounce was really there or I had taken a deeper step into the looney pool of Nutsville. I did have a lifetime membership, after all. I blinked and made fish faces for a few minutes as I tried to speak, but the words just came out as squeaks and sputter.

No one had ever come here. Jess didn't even come here. It was made to suppress me, control me, and purge me when I got too far out of control. I didn't think anyone besides me could come here, and it wasn't like I wanted to be here, I didn't have a choice. So seeing Bounce, the boss of us all and the head of the Breakers, standing in front of me? I have to say if I had a bladder, I probably would have peed my pants. Real badass, huh? Yeah. I know.

I swallowed hard as I pushed away from the wall, stepped forward, and looked up at him. He was the tallest of us all. Lean and powerful with medium-length hair that some said was blonde, some said was black, and others said they didn't know he had hair. Bounce could change his appearance with a thought. But his most common one was the one that stood before me now, which was lethal and clad in leather. He had the strangest eyes that changed colors like a mood ring. He usually kept them hidden behind his shades, but right now, I think he wanted me to see the color. It was red, and I may not be very smart, but red probably meant mad. Not good for me. At all.

"What do you mean, Bounce? My plans? Uh"—I looked around, smirked, and looked back—"sitting, and probably doing some standing. Then some more sitting. Then some standing. I can't really pace, itty-bitty space and all. Then maybe some sleep out of boredom."

He let out a growl, lip curling up to show some pretty wicked fangs of his own. "You know what I mean, Split. Why are you not doing your part? He's going insane."

Oh, that was great news. In fact, I had a big smile at the thought. "He is? Well, he put me away, so why don't you ask him?"

See, there are a few things you should never do.

Don't ever eat sushi from a gas station. Don't

ever wear leather pants without underwear. And don't ever cop an attitude with Bounce.

He had me pinned against the wall with a thought, and from our little chats on the outside, I had learned that struggling against Bounce's pin only made it tighter. So I just hung there, my boots tapping out a little rhythm as I hummed a little song. Eventually, we'd get to the point.

Hello? Head dweller on time-out? I was so good at waiting it out. It was an art.

I think it was my singing that finally made him let me go, which caused me to crash to the floor, letting out an "Ouuuuch."

Bounce glared at me, his nostrils flared with aggravation, his face tense with anger. "He can't handle it. He has never had to. He's losing it, and I need him. He had a purpose as a Breaker, and I can't have him out of control."

Oh, we couldn't have that. That might expose the whole hero badass game to the world. But I wasn't sure what Bounce was talking about. How come Jess couldn't handle it? He was big, strong, and powerful all on his own.

Okay, so maybe he was having some issues with pain and anger, but why couldn't he handle that?

I looked away, my lips going into a thin line, my jaw tight as I shook my head. "No. It's about time he handled what he does. What he makes happen." I snapped my eyes back to his. "I won't do it anymore. Not now. Not after what he did."

I said too much and slammed my mouth shut. Only Jess knew about Witch and me, and I was pretty sure it needed to stay that way. It was too messed up as it was.

Bounce let out a snarl and grabbed my shirt,

shaking me. "No. Not that. The insanity that created you is now driving Jess insane. It's the reason you were created, remember? To help him with it. He cannot handle it alone. He isn't equipped to."

That pissed me off. I grabbed Bounce's wrists—another unwise thing to do with Bounce—and yanked them off of me, pulling my shirt out of his hold. "You do not have to tell me about it. Maybe it's time he did handle it. I don't want to have just the bad and never the good, to have only the pain and nothing more."

Bounce came in low, baring his teeth, his face mottled with anger. "I need him. The world needs him. I don't know what happened between you two, but you need to get your shit straight. Figure out a way to work together."

"No!" I shoved him away and shook my head. "I won't do it. Not anymore!" I stepped up and met his eyes. "I may not have any rights, and I may not even really exist out there, but I can do this. I can refuse to help him. It's about time he handled his own life. Why should I help to save him? Save his life? I don't even have a life!"

I slammed my fist against my chest. "So, not even *you* can make me. You don't like it? He gets out of control? Please feel free to end him. That, I'll be happy to let you do. I won't stand in your way at all. Now if you don't mind, I do have a very active schedule."

I slid down the wall then pulled up my legs and wrapped my arms around my head as my forehead hit my knees. "Now, go. Please. Just go. You just don't understand. No one does. And no one cares."

My voice went soft as a whisper, full of pain. "I can't have just the bad and never the good." And never her. "Not anymore. I'm sorry."

I looked up, and Bounce was gone.

CHAPTER EIGHTEEN

The impossible option

You remember way up there, somewhere, where I said I made really bad decisions? This decision was looking like my worse ever and most likely my last. I was created for bad, pain, and violence, and because of that, I needed those things to exist. Not hard to figure out, right?

Yeah, but now that I wasn't doing those things for Jess, I was getting weaker and would be useless even if he did let me out or I chose to get out. The days blurred, interrupted by fits of Jess's rage, paranoia, and madness as he became more and more crazed by handling the insanity that he had never had to deal with before. All I could do was lay there and listen and wait for it all to end. And it would because the further out of control Jess became, the more Bounce would be faced with putting him down.

It had gone on for weeks, and the headspace was falling apart. Crumbling and cracking around me. The hole had never been colder as I lay curled up, shivering with teeth chattering, not even having enough energy to try to appeal to Jess. It would not have done me any good if I had—no one could reach him, and I was in his head. But he was finally feeling the insanity I had kept at bay since we were children so long ago. Seemed like forever since I had felt that cool grass that night.

Lifetimes ago.

I was lost in my memories, my side of our

mind teasing and soothing me with memories of Witch. Of her smile, her laugh, her touch, and of the one night we had shared. It was misery, however, as I cried out her name and wished to see her one more time. To kiss those beautiful lips and just curl up and lose myself in the haven of her arms.

"Sundown."

I cracked open my eyes, the pain and weakness making that seem like the hardest task ever. My voice was hoarse, weak, and barely there. "Bounce?"

Bounce let out a long breath and tilted his head to look at me. "I wish you had listened to me. Now it may be too late. You're both stubborn idiots."

I gave a weak grin and shrugged my shoulders. "And he's the smartest one. Or used to be."

Pain hit me, and I curled up tighter. It felt like I was starving, but then again, I guess I was. The strength I had been using not to be drawn out by Jess's pain and suffering had taken its toll. And without feeding my need for violence and pain, I was literally dying of starvation of the weirdest kind.

"I have a solution. One that will end this."

I frowned and looked up, gasping through the pain. "End? A solution?"

It didn't make any sense. Did he mean end Jess? I found that hard to believe. He was a hero, and Bounce used him for so many things. Oh, wait.

"Oh. Uh, you mean end me."

Bounce took a seat on the floor across from me, bringing up a knee and draping an arm on it, his fingers slowly tapping as if counting down a timer no one else could hear. He shrugged and looked away. "You wanted it to end. I can give you that. But I would like to try to save you both." His gaze returned to me.

"What do you have to lose? Either I can save you, or it ends. Either way, does it matter?"

I thought about that and struggled to sit up. "You said you could save us both. I won't do this anymore. I can't. If you mean going back to the way it was, then no. Ending it is better."

Another wave of pain hit me, and I saw Bounce's mouth move but couldn't hear him through it. I blinked and frowned. "What did you say?" Because there was no way I heard him right.

He gave me a stone-cold look and repeated it. "I said, what if I can give you your own body. Your own life?"

Okay, so I had heard it right. But my brain refused to believe it. I gawked, or at least thought I did, but I know I blinked. Like many, many times. "What are you talking about? How can you do that?"

Bounce looked away. "With the help of an old friend." He looked back at me. "I can't guarantee it will work. You may very well end, but you wanted it to end, so you may get your wish." He stood and looked down at me. "What do you say? Do I attempt it?"

I looked up at him, wondering if I had ended and this was some weird dream or some strange trick of my dead brain. But I don't think dead brains can play tricks. Can they? Oh, wait, anyway, back to Bounce. Sorry.

I narrowed my eyes, doubt and fear swimming up through the pain. Maybe it was a trick, which wouldn't surprise me one bit. I grimaced in pain and rubbed my hands over my face, gritting my teeth as I tried to focus on the right words. "What does Jess say? Did you ask? And I would have my own life? Body and everything?" I pointed a shaking finger. "As a human thing, right? I don't want to be like a lizard or a kitten or something."

Hey, don't laugh. I had no idea what Bounce could do. So, you gotta cover the bases. Think beyond the immortal box. Could you imagine being a lizard for the rest of your life? An immortal reptile? That would probably suck. Not to mention getting smooshed under someone's boot. With my luck? That would happen within hours.

Bounce gave me a look of bafflement and shook his head. "You are just so fucking strange." He got to his feet and leaned against the wall. "Your own life. With your own human body. But it comes with a price."

I rolled my eyes. Of course, it came with a price. Everything always did. Nothing was free except for what you don't want—like cancer, pimples, or other bad things. Letting my gaze go back to his as another spasm of pain hit me, causing me to hiss until it passed, I said with a groan, "Price? What is it?"

Bounce leveled a serious look at me, one that was even colder than the air that blew around us. "You have to keep the madness and deal with it. I cannot separate it from you as it is what created you. So if I can give you your own existence, you must exist together with it."

I glared at him. Well, glared as much as one could while shivering, groaning, and wishing for it all to stop. "Wait. Who drives? I better be the damn driver, Bounce. I will never go back to being the dark side. So okay, but I drive. I'm in charge of me—for once."

I gave it more thought and pointed a finger that shook badly, so not as threatening as I had wanted. Oh, well. I was ceasing to exist. "New life. No one knows what I used to be. A fresh start. That or no deal. We die."

Bounce gave one quick sharp nod, but something about it seemed, well, off. But I was too far gone to question it. I wish I had.

I thought about all that he had said, what all it meant, frowning as the intensity of mulling it over creased my brow, and I wrapped my arms around myself. "And what does Jess say?" I looked up at him. "He was asked, right?"

Bounce's face turned grave as he looked away, slid on his shades once more, and said flatly, "He wants you gone. He is willing to die to make it so." He looked back at me, bared his fangs, and shook his head with a heavy sigh. "He suffers as much as you do. He just wants it to stop."

To say that hurt, despite the resentment and the hate, was a huge understatement. I don't know, but I guess the part of me that used to be his best friend and almost like a brother still lived somewhere deep inside. I looked down at the ground and stared at Bounce's boots. Why were they scuffed? He was a god of something with huge powers. After all, he created all the Breakers, and it was rumored he did so to avenge a family that was slaughtered by the Energy Eaters, but no one really knew for sure. So why would he ever have worn-out, scuffed-up boots? Couldn't he just go *poof* and make those mars, blemishes, and scratches disappear? Or make a new pair that was perfect with just a thought? Or at least buy some at Costco. That just confused me, and I got fixated on those defects for a few minutes.

Bounce said my name quietly.

I looked up, met those shaded eyes, and said in defeat, "I'll do it." I really hoped I turned out better than those boots.

C H A P T E R   N I N E T E E N

Bad pain

Pain.

Now, to most people, pain is something to be avoided and not something they relish, enjoy, or need. But I am not most people, probably because I'm technically not a people or uh, person. I know. I told you it's complicated.

But to me, pain empowers, strengthens and gives me the freedom to be in control, in charge, and out. It makes me clear and focused, and nothing can take me down while I stand and fight.

But that was before Bounce carried out his plan.

By the time it all took place, I was so weak I couldn't even scream. I was barely conscious as I lay there, curled up, sweating, and cold, gasping for air that was rushing out of the cracks of Jess's headspace and away from me. I felt like a goldfish unable to flop anymore and doing nothing more than gasping, mouth open, trying to draw in water that wasn't there.

God, this plan sucked. I really hoped Bounce was better at decisions than I was. *Please, please, don't let me be boots. Or a reptile.*

I was at the point where all I could do was spasm and shiver when something changed. It was like someone plugged in a view to Jess's outside again as I was getting small, brief glimpses, filled with static of what was going on.

Opening my eyes when the sound registered, I

saw Bounce. He was standing with a woman. A tall, lean, beautiful woman who looked exotic, and yet there was no way to know what ethnic background she was. All of them? None of them? She was so beautiful yet so tough looking that you really wanted to figure it out or run. But it was her eyes, which were so intense and seemed to be looking at me. Not Jess.

Me.

Her hair was black, but then it seemed pink? Wait—no, black. Maybe? Shaking my head weakly, hoping to clear it, I blinked as tears blurred my vision. I tried to focus on what they were saying as I was only getting bits and pieces through the static.

"… but this will make it harder to keep him hidden."

Bounce was pacing and seemed almost agitated at her words as he glared back at her, pointing.

"And the alternative is any better? We destroy them both? Destiny is a bitch, and she will bitch-slap us harder if we don't even try."

I frowned and struggled to sit—which, by the way, got me nowhere. But trying counts for something, right? What were they talking about? My brain stopped and started, short-circuiting by the minute and fading fast.

The woman smiled at him, but nothing about it seemed to say she was amused or that she was going to say something ha-ha. "Well, whose fault is it that destiny has been tampered with, Bounce? Not mine. You and your obsession with chasing that which destroyed what you loved has gotten us into this mess. And now you want my help? I am tempted to give you the finger and watch it all fall apart."

She looked at me again. No, wait, she had to

be looking at Jess, but it seemed like she was looking into my eyes as if she knew I was there. They had to be talking about Jess because I knew he was destined for something big. Right? I had felt that since the moment I was aware.

Bounce snarled. "Something changed. He broke rules that were never even thought of. That is not my fault. We have to save him."

Yep, Jess. Because it was always about Jess. He was the hero, the one everyone wanted. Jess was the one that made a difference in life and did good things for mankind. I didn't matter, and I never had until they thought they were going to be losing their big, bad hero. But I was only a means to an end and nothing more.

I closed my eyes and waited until my water wasn't coming back and the hidden goldfish I was no longer had a bowl.

Then the pain hit.

It bloomed in my head like a small razor cut. Sharp and precise and I gasped, but then that razor sliced deep, and the pain went from just a bloom to an explosion of immense proportions.

At first, I screamed, the sound just a hiss of air—air I didn't have. But soon, the pain defied even that, and my screams were loud, hysterical, and desperate. I seized and thrashed, clawing at my head as the pain ripped and shredded.

Through the haze of anguish, I heard another scream. Jess.

For the first time, his pain had the opposite effect on me. Rather than having to fight to be drawn out, it was making me feel like I was being pulled further in. I fought against it, clawing at the floor until my nails broke and bled. Bounce had said I could have my own life.

Or he would end me.

I was starting to realize that this was my end. It had all been a trick, a ploy to save Jess. And as much as I had wanted that, I now wanted the opposite. Oh, god. I would never see my Witch again, even if it was through Jess's eyes. I had been so stupid.

My screams became laced with pleas, begging, and promises that I would be good. That I would obey the rules and do whatever they wanted me to do. But it was too late.

Destiny.

That single word spoken by a strange damn voice, somehow, now got through the haze of agony. I lay there, curled up tight, blood streaming down my fingers from them gouging into my head and clawing at the crumbling walls as I tried to make it stop hurting and to stay, and I screamed, "Destiny? What destiny? Who are you?"

Soon.

Then the pain expanded, snapped, and I shattered into a hundred-million pieces with a scream that imploded the headspace, sending the pieces into dust and darkness.

And silence. Gone.

C H A P T E R   T W E N T Y

Sock soup

"**D**rink."

I cracked my eye open, the other was pressed against a floor, and through blurred vision, I saw a chipped china bowl.

"Drink."

My eye drifted up to see the face of a tiny Asian man. He had a handlebar mustache that seemed at odds with his ancient face. His eyes were so dark they appeared black with little white showing. He looked both hundreds of years old and ageless, like Botox didn't stand a chance nor was it needed.

My gaze went back to the bowl, and I frowned. I thought about reaching for it, but nothing was happening. Then a hand in my line of sight reached out to take it. I thought it might be mine, but I didn't feel it. It was trembling so bad that it never made it to the bowl.

I was hit with pain so overwhelming that the bowl got hit by that thrashing hand and shattered as blackness came in and took me away.

"Drink."

Sometime must have passed because when my eyes opened this time, I was staring up at a yellowed and cracked ceiling. But it was like I was looking at it through a telescope, narrowed and focused on just one spot surrounded by smooth darkness. I turned my head and swallowed, once again seeing a bowl sitting in my line of sight on the floor. And that small Asian man, who was smiling, with yellowed teeth that matched the ceiling above, motioned with a small, twisted hand to the bowl.

"Drink."

I swallowed and rolled to my side, that weird delay once again making it happen seconds later than when I had thought to do it. I focused on the bowl, and again, a hand reached out to take it, but it felt weird. Like I was watching the hand but not feeling it. It fumbled, still shaking, but somehow made it to the bowl.

The man smiled and motioned with his hands to form what looked like a bowl. He then brought his imaginary bowl to his lips, those deep, black eyes nailing me with intensity as I followed his actions like some strange puppet show.

When the man reached out to help lift my head—that too felt disconnected—there was no sensation as the bowl lifted to my mouth. It was like looking at old dishwater, brown and cloudy with what looked like herbs and other chunks floating in it.

I took a sip, and the moment I did, nausea hit me, triggering my gag reflex, and I spewed soup and bile all over both of us. I choked and curled up to vomit, great heaves that felt like I was ralphing up my guts.

The Asian man wiped his face and mumbled, "Not ready."

And darkness snagged me again.

"Drink."

Again with the drink?

Again with my eyes opening. I was on my stomach as I rolled my eyes up to look at the cracked china bowl in front of me, and the Asian man was squatting beyond that, watching. This time, I was able to roll and sit, and while it happened with a delay, it was only a second, maybe two, so that was better. I also felt the floor underneath my ass, and as I reached out, I made contact with the bowl even though the hand was still shaking.

The little man kept watching, a gleeful smile cracking his lips, his small tongue licking his teeth and clucking as he did. I kept my eyes on him as I lifted the bowl and drank. It tasted like old socks brewed with dirt and mold, but suddenly, I was so thirsty, so hungry, I downed it, dripping it down my chin and onto my chest, licking the bowl for more.

He laughed and clapped and then did the strangest little dance around me, making me dizzy as I tried to track him with eyes that seemed to be delayed, too.

He did a few rounds around me, clucking and cackling, before coming to a stop in front of me. He babbled in what I guessed was Chinese, or my brain was fried because I didn't understand a word.

"Can I have a shower, please?" Whoa. Who was that? Wait, was that my voice?

It was hoarse and strained, but I could tell it was different than any I had heard before. Which meant, not Jess's voice—his voice was a deep baritone with a southern drawl, but this one was more a tenor with no drawl, and soft, and it sounded so foreign to me even though it was obviously mine now.

The little man nodded and beckoned me to follow. Again, there was that delay, but I made it to my feet, swaying, and feeling dizzy as the room seemed to spin before it passed. I followed like a drunken person as he led me to a small bathroom. Dingy, old, and tiny, but clean. He motioned to some clothes sitting on the tank of the commode and then closed the door behind him.

I looked around, and that was when I saw, well, me.

I blinked and frowned, tilting my head to see a total stranger in the cracked, speckled mirror. I looked nothing like Jess. Jess had a rugged look, tough yet handsome, that women loved. This face? The one looking back at me? Wasn't rugged or tough looking. The nose was little too big, but the face had a nice look, I guess. I brought a hand up to rub at the growth of whiskers on my jaw, touching the full lips and rubbing over the planes of my features.

Again, there was that delay in both action and sensation as I ran my hand through hair, which was soft brown and didn't seem to want to lie down and behave. My fingers brushed over a wound in the back of my head, sore and closed with jagged stitches. I pulled my hand away and met my eyes. My own eyes.

They, too, were different than Jess's eyes, which were a deep brown. These—wait, my eyes were a bright brilliant blue. Almost too bright as I brought my hand back up to pull down my bottom eyelid to search those azure depths, amazed to know I was looking at myself. It was so surreal, so strange.

I brought my fingers down to get to know the rest of my face, coming to terms with that small delay, hoping it would get better but not caring if it didn't.

I curled my lips and pulled up the top one with my fingers to find fangs. Oh, cool. I kinda like fangs. It would be easier to be a badass because this face was not the face of a stone-cold killer. Not anymore.

That was when I saw the mark, and I moved my hand to stare at the Breaker stamp on my left forearm.

It was how Bounce's secret army of Breakers

and the human branch called Relays, recognized each other. Breakers had the full stamp, Relays had just the center detail, and those aligned with Bounce had other parts and pieces of it. Jess's was on his shoulder, and mine was now on my arm. I smiled at that. Mine.

My arm. My face, my hands, my body.

I smiled and admitted that it was a nice smile.

But I'd have to make sure to hide the fangs around humans.

I stepped back to look at myself. I had the usual muscular physique that all Breakers had when they were turned, lean and ripped muscle, but I was a bit smaller than Jess and the others. I didn't care about that either. I got a puzzled frown when my fingers grazed a nasty cut from my gut to my chest. It was healing, as Breakers healed pretty fast, and just like my head, it had a zig-zag stitch job that would leave a scar. We always had scars to remind us of what we had done to get them.

I thought I was a bit shorter, too. All the Breakers topped six feet and above with some topping eight feet, but it was hard to tell next to Mr. Handlebar Asian guy out there. It was like standing next to a yard gnome, so anyone would be tall.

Okay, I admit it—oh, come on, you would have too—I looked way down and let out a laugh. Yeah, I was hung, which was a nice thing to find. I went from being afraid of being an immortal lizard or a pair of boots to wondering if I had the parts of the former and was relieved to find I didn't. Tilting my head to look down at it, I grasped it and said, "Don't worry, buddy. You and I will get to know each other really well."

It amused me that it took a few seconds to feel the sensation of my cock in my hand. But boy, was I glad I wasn't made like a Ken doll.

Stepping into the shower, almost tripping due to that send-and-receive issue, I turned on the taps, and the pipes groaned and sputtered as the water hit me, cold and welcome.

I still felt disconnected due to that pause in the nerves, but I was getting used to it. I scrubbed with some strange soap that was handmade and made my skin tingle, which was not all that unpleasant. I used it on my hair, too, hissing in pain as my fingers couldn't help but probe the healing wound in my head. I wondered who had this body before I did.

And who the hell did they piss off? Their loss, my gain.

Finishing up, I dried off and took my time getting to know the new me—long, lean legs and the same brown hair with a dusting of it in all the correct places. I turned to look in the mirror and noticed a really nice ass, if that wasn't too weird for me to say about my own ass. But it's a really nice one, so why not. And hey, no back hair. Win-win.

Smiling, I slipped on the old T-shirt, probably from one of the thrift shops that dotted the whole city because I didn't see the little Asian man being a University of Kentucky basketball fan. After stepping into jogging sweats, throwing a hand out against the wall to keep from falling over as my balance was still wonky, I walked out and stopped to see Bounce standing there. He rolled his gaze to me, stopping his chat with the Asian man—talking in that language I couldn't understand—and he gave a slight smile. He never really smiled, not that I remembered, so I guess a half smile was better than none.

Bounce turned to face me, crossing his arms on his chest. "So. What now?"

I smiled, tilted my head, and replied, "Where is she?"

SNEAK PEEK AT BOOK TWO IN THE GRID SERIES:

MADNESS

Available Now!

CHAPTER ONE

One second later and Reno would have been adding his blood to the Eater goo that slicked the pavement. Bowing his back as the blade sliced forward, he grabbed the wrist of the nasty thing trying to slice and dice him to use its momentum to pull it forward. He then brought his elbow down hard at the base of its skull, shattering bone, muscle and sending it into the pool of foul smelling ooze.

Spinning around, bleeding from a half dozen cuts and slices, he was disappointed to find that the fun was over.

So far he didn't hear any sirens so that was always a good thing as he took in the dark and dank Reno, Nevada alley. The dark space between the buildings was now decorated with a dozen demonic piles turning into thick gruesome puddles that were once Energy Eaters. Once killed, these demons straight out of Hell were no longer able to maintain their human form and since they weren't able to survive long in their true forms outside Hell, they turned into well… liquefied bad, smelly jelly looking stuff. It smelled bad. It felt bad. And it tasted ten times worse than the other two combined. What could he say? Reno was really messy when he had fun.

Reaching into his back pocket to pull out a Twizzler, he then slapped it on his tongue. He crinkled up his face as he tried not to smell the stench or look too close at the slaughtered bodies as they melted away.

It wasn't pretty. At all. It was like that ooze at the bottom of a forgotten dumpster that had sat in the sun way too long.

Some of the other Breakers had Relays who could come in and clean up the mess left behind from dispatching the Energy Eaters or, sadly, any bodies of human fatalities the demons left behind.

Their usual victims were women and sometimes children, the weak that scared easily. The higher the level of fear and panic of the victim the more empowered their spark would glow. It became more supercharged than pop rock candy with adrenaline and endorphins to fuel the fear.

The stronger the spark, the longer the demons could exist in the human world. Feeding on that allowed the Eaters to exist here topside, because Hell wasn't exactly known as a party place. So their sole goal was living here among the humans on Earth. He had heard they weren't very welcome in Hell at all.

But, as he watched the mess transform into a water-like substance, he wasn't one of those lucky Breakers. He was still 'on probation' with the god who created as well as managed the Breakers. That god was called Bounce. It was Bounce who waited at the gates of Hell, and paid for each of their souls.

Why Hell? Well, each Breaker had been a bad, very bad, or the worst kind of human, and if Bounce bought them they in turn got a second chance to redeem themselves and, if they were lucky, get a chance to live again by doing it right. It's not like a soul had many options—it was being a Breaker or burning up forever in the hellfire.

It wasn't without its price however. It meant your soul was basically in hock to Hell and Bounce was like the lien-holder, making sure you made your payments. Only he could decide when the debt was paid, but it had some cool bonuses as well.

Breakers were ten times stronger than any human could hope to be, faster too. They healed super-fast and were immortal, which meant they couldn't die from natural causes. Only beheading or bleeding out could kill them. Along with that, being a Breaker paid really well, so, all in all? A Breaker was a total bad-ass.

A Breaker's sole purpose was to wipe the Energy Eaters off the realm of mankind, but how the Energy Eaters walked the Earth and why was the stuff of legend. Like a really dark and scary fairy tale with the happy ending seeming very far away.

Being a Breaker wasn't without its risks and downfalls. There was the whole beheading and dying thing for one. Another was being tied to Hell, you couldn't walk in the light of day.

Then there was the point system - for each human they failed to save it was like points against the Breaker. Too many points or not following the rules would mean Bounce would live up to his nickname and bounce your soul right back to Hell to burn for eternity. Second chance done and over.

All served the Grid and Reno knew even less about the logistics of it all. He had never really asked. Reno only knew that the Grid kept mankind's energy strong and served to keep everything balanced. Balanced, that is, until the Great Light could wipe out darkness and restore faith to mankind to be good for all time.

No one, he didn't think, knew what the Great Light was. Many were beginning to think it was a false prophecy and was never going to happen.

Reno had never really asked about how the

war had started but he had heard that the demons were made to feed on the light of mankind and destroy it. To eventually wipe out the species and make a very nasty Hell on Earth. Some said that Lucifer's own son was driven mad with revenge and created them.

The demons fed on mankind like a starving dude in an all-you-can-eat buffet and only left behind an empty shell with no chance for the person who owned it to have redemption or be judged by Heaven.

Because Earth was a lot more fun than Hell, where they were treated like freaks and strays. The demons really wanted to claim the Earth realm as their new home so they wouldn't have to go back to their own. Feeding off humans was their extended stay ticket to do that.

Reno didn't care about all that. He just did his job even though he wasn't really sure who was winning the war because it had been going on as long as there had been a Heaven and Hell, but he didn't mind. In fact, he never really complained or took anything for granted.

He was, after all, only three years old.

It seemed like much longer than that. But it wasn't. Three years ago he had been just a split personality of one of the most heroic and honorable Breakers by the name of Jess Bailey. The same insanity that had caused Jess's personality to split for survival was the same one that drove the hero insane. It had been Reno's job to make sure that didn't happen to Jess by controlling the insanity, by being a buffer between it and the hero to handle all the bad that the hero couldn't deal with.

He had to take all the pain and violence, all

the bad that had started when Jess was just a little boy of seven years old.

He had never complained about that either…well okay, maybe every once in a while. But it was his only purpose and the only reason for his existence, so he rarely questioned it.

Until her.

Emma.

His Witch.

Then all bets were off on what he would do or not do, with the latter being the problem. He had refused to help Jess any longer and that insanity all but destroyed the hero. He had suffered too as they both declined and deteriorated into insanity. But it was bound to happen.

Imagine watching the man who he had come to hate, after more than a century of letting him out only to handle the bad and kept him in a place they both called 'the Hole', be with the one woman they both loved?

The Hole was black, windy and cold; all designed to put him in his place and purge evil urges inside of Jess's very strong telepathic mind. And Reno hated it. But he hated it more after Jess became involved with Emma because Jess decided the best torture of all was to make Reno watch their relationship.

Every. Single. Thing.

Yes, even their sex life.

All from inside of Jess's head.

By design, Reno was never supposed to have positive feelings or emotions of being good and right. The things that made life worth fighting for like compassion, love, kindness and made someone want to be good. Emotions Reno had never felt, developed or gave a damn about because he thought they made a person weak. His job was to be ruthless and strong.

But Emma had changed all that in one night.

He never knew what or who had helped him out that night to be able to drive and be in control of the body he and Jess shared, but he really hoped he got a chance to thank them.

That one night of passion with Emma had changed him and he knew there was no going back.

He had never been kissed by a woman before, nor touched. He had never had sex and she had been his first and his only.

He had never been allowed those things before because they were good things and only Jess was allowed those. He was only allowed the bad.

From that one night, those foreign but good emotions took root and grew and sealed the pain that would cause his and Jess's split to rip wide open.

But Emma never knew it was Reno she had shared that first night with and not Jess because of their shared body.

Jess had then used that to have a relationship that had lasted for months. With the woman his split dark-side had fallen completely and totally in love with. Maybe from the first moment Reno had seen her.

But Jess wasn't going to let Reno forget who was in charge and that was why the torture of watching them together was meant to be a lesson. It was a lesson all right. A lesson on how to hate even more than Reno had before.

So for months, he sat as he was shown when Emma and Jess laughed, kissed, and worse of all made love. He was given the view without mercy and had to hear the sounds even when he wrapped his arms around his head to block them, begging for Jess to stop.

Resentment had already grown thick between them long ago, so hate grew strong and unbreakable in that foundation. He had taken that torture and did his purpose as always, hating it more and more, because even if it was through Jess's eyes at least he could still see Emma. Albeit making sure to inflict pain and injury as a reminder for when Jess regained control.

Reno called her Witch because when they met that perfect night, he didn't know her name and was unsure what Jess had told her, as Jess had met her first. The two halves did not often share experiences like they once had as children so he had no idea what had transpired between her and Jess. So, as a cover, he chose a nickname of what she was in life— Witch.

All of that seemed to have no end in sight until Jess made a fatal mistake that would bring destruction to their joined existence forever.

Jess broke Emma's heart.

Reno had never learned why, because without warning or reason, Jess stopped showing him…well anything. He had begged and pleaded for Jess to at least show him how she was, even if it ripped his heart apart to be a back seat driver in their love affair. But rather than get his plea, he was locked away even tighter than before and had literally been kept in the dark for months in The Hole.

So Reno was pushed to do the one thing he had never even dared to even contemplate before. Ignore his purpose, sit back and do nothing.

It had not taken long for Jess to be overtaken by the insanity he had kept at bay from the hero for over a century. The plan took its toll on Reno as well. Since he was a part of Jess's mind, as it deteriorated so did the head space he was contained in. He had gotten weaker and became less substance the further Jess slipped into insanity. But Reno didn't care.

They would both be destroyed and at least his torturous existence would end. And if they were gone, Jess could never hurt his Witch again.

It had been almost over, with him too weak to even speak or move in the small, dark and cold head space, when Bounce had offered him the one thing he had never even thought was possible.

Reno would have his own life with his own body.

Sure, it was to save Jess since the hero was all anyone cared about, but Reno had grabbed at that chance.

Jess had more than happily agreed as they hated each other enough. There were no promises it would work but at least Jess would be freed of the insanity, and of him. *Reno's* existence was the one at risk as Bounce would do anything to save one of his Breakers and he wasn't even a whole being.

But it had worked with the help of an ancient Asian man by the name of Mr. Hahn. And when Bounce asked him after the transition what he wanted with his new life, the answer for Reno had been simple. His own life; one with no one knowing what or who he used to be or who he had been a part of. A fresh.

And now three years later, after months of getting used to a body that still had delays, when his mind told it to do one thing and it sometimes responded a split second later, he had been assigned to Reno, Nevada.

The rumors of Jess's 'Sundown' side had been whispered about. That the seemingly perfect hero had a flaw. A dark side that the man called Sundown, which did the most brutal and violent deeds needed. Little did they know how true those rumors were, for he was Jess's Sundown side; it was the name the little boy had given his dark half when they first became joined in destiny.

Reno didn't want anyone to know, and be judged for that past, or think he was a freak. Not to mention Jess was never told how successful Bounce's little experiment had been with the help of both Mr. Hahn and a woman he still didn't know anything about.

The excruciating pain of the separation was a distant memory, like some say that of childbirth or just a shadow in the back of his mind.

But Reno remembered it being bad, as in the worst of the bad that he had ever felt. And that was saying something.

So Bounce had agreed and as far as anyone knew, even to Jess, he had ceased to exist that day. Jess had recovered and became one of Bounce's enforcers and a true heroic bad-ass. And Reno had been sent to Reno, Nevada, a Breaker now in his own right with the brand proudly scarred on his left forearm. But the brand was so much more than that. It was a direct connection to the Grid.

The 'stamp', as the Breakers called the brand, was made up of evolving, tiny nano-bots of energy. They could feed back how the Breaker was doing, when they were in danger, even the locale to be pinpointed and be tracked.

They called it going online. And a simple thumb print press that was encrypted and encoded on the Grid was all it took for a Breaker to do so. That brand also showed a secret fellowship to members of the city who worked covertly for the Grid. Kept hidden otherwise from the very realm of mankind in which they fought to save.

Reno was proud of being a Breaker, of being a hero like Jess. He had done his job and done it well, as night after night he took on dozens of Energy Eaters without backup or help like the other Breakers. He was grateful for the chance given to him and didn't want to ruin his one chance so he obeyed every rule.

Without question and without complaint. Again.

It worked out well for him as it served a dual purpose. He was able to feed the nature of what he was—a creature of pain and violence—and do his job of Eater-goo-be-gone.

It fulfilled his duty as a Breaker and it fed the need to still have pain and violence in his existence. It was as needed as breathing so he made sure it stayed happy. Since insanity had caused his creation when Jess's psyche had split as that little human boy, he couldn't be split from it when he transitioned to his own body. So now that same insanity was his to deal with. It was no longer Jess's burden to hide and be buffered from, but Reno's.

Due to that, and developing a 'good side', he now was a split of his own. Light and dark had to exist together so just like Jess; he too had a Sundown side. One he could tap, just like Jess, to handle the worst pain and violence.

But unlike Jess, he treated it well, and they shared in everything. Always seeing and feeling whatever he saw and experienced. No way was he going to treat his dark side like Jess had treated him.

Not that the side was needed very often. He made sure to never let himself tap on the border that kept the madness at bay. The reason for that was that as much as he was still amazed that Bounce had parked him in his new body, he was also scared he could somehow break the connection. Cause too much damage and his split essence would somehow be snapped from its supernatural connection with a body it had not been created to be in and his only chance with it. So he took precautions out of that fear to not go too dangerous and dark.

Like the sugar. He always had candy on him, and strawberry licorice rope was his candy of choice. It dissolved slowly and was durable even when he fidgeted with it in his fangs or was fighting. Sugar seemed to quiet the constant buzz he had in his head almost as if the sweetness dampened the insanity by changing the chemistry in his brain.

He didn't really know actually why or how, only that it worked. So as long as he had violence or pain, and candy, he was level and in good shape.

But back to the yucky task at hand…

As the thick gel began to sluice into the city's drainage system, Reno squatted down with the licorice rope spinning in his lips, to put a finger in the tar black and red mess.

He grinned as he drew a happy face in it, being sure to draw a tongue at the side of the mouth. He got bored waiting for it all to turn to liquid so he was always looking for a way to waste the time.

Reno was mostly happy and you were supposed to share that. Even with goo.

That was about to change.

CHAPTER TWO

"**W**hat the Pac-Man are you doing?"

He was still squatted down watching his former happy face become a sad face as it turned into the water stuff when he heard the god Bounce's voice behind him. Looking over his shoulder, Reno smiled and looked back down. "I don't know. I figure it didn't smile much and should go out happy." He stood and wiped his Eater goo covered hand on his jeans as he turned to face Bounce.

Bounce rolled his eyes, snorted and pointed, not appearing amused at the puddle. "They go back to Hell, Reno. They probably do not find that a happy prospect."

Reno frowned as he pursed his lips left and right to look back down at the Eater slick. "Oh, uh, I didn't really think about that part."

Reno knew he wasn't really the smartest of Breakers and had never been good at decisions.

That had gotten him into all this, so maybe it was a mix of good and bad just like him. Bounce had named him Reno, which was fine, because a lot of Breakers adopted the city they were assigned to when they were first turned. Reno had never had a name other than Sundown so he had no problem with the new moniker. It had stuck, and he kind of liked it.

His frown deepened as he rolled his gaze to Bounce's, whose eyes were hidden behind dark shades even now in the dark of night.

No one really knew what Bounce was. There were all kinds of legends and whispers about that too.

All that was really known was that the god was uber-powerful, ancient, and could change his appearance to be anyone or no one in a blink.

Bounce's eyes were like a mood ring in the fact that they changed depending on whatever mood the god was in. But they all knew he held their existence in his moods and his grasp so the Breakers both respected and feared that.

He was taller than most with a lean muscled physique and olive skin with intense, but super-model perfect features. Some said he was Oriental while others said Polynesian. But Bounce never said. And no one dared to ask.

Even Reno wasn't that stupid.

Reno did know the god had a very odd fixation on the eighties right down to the vintage t-shirts Bounce always wore. The man actually could make the Thriller jacket he was wearing now along with a Ms. Pac-Man t-shirt look deadly. Toss in the mint-condition Air Jordans and Bounce had a certain style. The eighties never looked so cool.

As the Eater ooze had finally liquefied into nothing more than water, Reno couldn't help but wonder why Bounce was here as he did an internal mental double-check.

He had made sure to obey all the rules and procedures and as far as he knew, careful not to break a single one. His human losses were a big count of zero and he made sure he always dropped the injured off at the hospital and never the morgue.

And even if the fighting took place right in front them, the humans never remembered any of it. A side effect of the Eater's bite was it contained which caused the human to forget an incident once the feeding had begun. It actually benefited the

Breakers and helped keep it all hidden much to the Eaters' frustration.

He stood next to Bounce, crossing his arms as he spun the Twizzler faster in his fangs to cut the god a sideways glance.

"Am I in trouble or something? I mean, uh, I've been doing good right?"

Bounce looked over and nodded. Actually Reno was exceptional at his job. His tallies were the highest of any of the new initiated Breakers and higher than even some of the senior ones. The young Breaker never complained or bitched about anything for the man truly did not take a solitary thing for granted.

Bounce had also learned that Reno donated a large portion of his income which was pro-athlete salary size to the local homeless shelters and shelters for abused women and children.

It wasn't a requirement that the Breakers give anything back to society other than protect it and Bounce was unsure why Reno did, but it amazed the god all the same. Not that he let Reno or anyone know that, for he was not one to loosen his much feared grip on his soldiers.

"Let's go back to your place, Reno. We need to talk." Bounce saw the man's look of fear and calmly shook his head. "No, you are not in trouble and you have done nothing wrong."

As they walked, he knew Reno was worried, as would any Breaker be. But considering Reno's past and the man's deep-seated need to make sure he did right to keep his existence, he knew that Reno's worry was far more justified than the rest.

Reno unlocked the downstairs of a stairwell that led to a small apartment above a coffee shop.

Despite the fact the Breaker made millions, he still lived in an efficiency apartment that some would call a rat hole and some would note it down next on a list to condemn.

Walking into the small space, Reno tossed his gear on the door side table to let Bounce walk in and closed the door behind them.

"Uh, there's a chair. You can have it. I'll stand."

There was indeed a chair along with a blanket covered pallet on the floor along with a small TV with a cable box sitting on a milk crate most likely from the coffee shop below.

There were no other rooms but a kitchenette that consisted of a hot plate and a small fridge that stood in one corner with a small shower and toilet in the opposite corner.

Reno knew it was a plain apartment with not a single sign of the money and power of the Breaker who lived here. But Reno didn't care. He was used to simple and small, and besides, he couldn't think of anything he really wanted money-wise. His only splurge was paying for cable so he could watch his cartoons.

Reno loved cartoons regardless of the time they were made. The classics, the modern ones, Disney or Nickelodeon; it didn't matter, he loved them all. He figured it was because he had never had a childhood of his own. If he did? He so would have watched cartoons constantly.

Bounce eyed the chair as if doubting its ability to hold his size or weight but chanced it as he sat down anyway. It did give a groan of protest and Reno could not help but let out a snicker as Bounce almost gingerly brought an ankle to his knee.

"Why don't you get a nicer place, Reno?"

He shrugged at the god's question and went over to the fridge and pulled out a juice pouch and stabbed a straw in it. "Want one?"

Bounce smirked and shook his head no.

Okay, fine. Reno didn't really drink beer and he was a sucker for the juice and the Kool-Aid ones too. He loved the things and maybe Bounce didn't, but with Reno's need for sugar he never liked the usual beer or other drinks of the others. The more sugar the better.

Walking over to pick up his gear holster on the entry table that held twin XD 9mm's and daggers, Reno went to the curtain that cornered off one end of the room acting as a closet for storage. Just a few clothes, but dozens and dozens of coffee cans. So many that they toppled and he had to catch them as he tried to hang his gear belt up. One rolled and landed in front of Bounce, stopped by the god's boot resting on it to end its continued escape across the floor.

Bounce bent down and picked the can up, a brow arching as he pried the plastic lid off. It was packed full of cash to the brim that was so tightly packed it seemed to test the integrity of the metal can's seam. He looked up at Reno. "You're keeping your pay in cans?"

Reno opened his mouth to speak as he juggled the cans trying to revolt and stood back, hands braced for them to fall again as he restored them back to messy columns. He glanced over at Bounce and looked back at the stacked cans.

"Well, I don't really spend it but to pay rent and food. And uh, cable. But I give a can a week to the shelters. They don't know it's me as I just leave the can in the donation box. The cans keep the money dry and make it easy to carry. And the shop gives me the cans for free."

He had been told not to drink coffee as it made him so hyper he was a danger to himself. The one time he did it had been scary and Bounce slapped that rule on him. Something about squirrels should never be allowed to suck on crack rocks nor Reno coffee.

He had all kinds of rules that made him different than the others, but he didn't care if Bounce put a million rules on him if it meant he had his own life.

He walked over and took the one can Bounce held and added it to the rest and then pulled the curtain closed. That's when he gave it too much thought and his eyes widened to look over at Bounce. What if donating his pay was wrong and he had just screwed up by telling Bounce. Or, maybe Bounce already knew and that's why he was here.

Reno spoke in a very quiet voice as he pointed at the curtain as if he was waiting for the reprimand or even worse, punishment.

"I make sure I don't let anyone see me. But uh, I kinda know what it's like is to be without a home in the cold and dark so that's why I donate some of my pay."

"Good job, just keep putting our heads in a noose. Would you like me to knit us a scarf to cover the bruise? Shut. Up."

He winced as his dark side decided to point out in his head that he wasn't making Bounce's job very hard by babbling on and on as he looked over at the god.

"I checked the rules and it didn't say anything

against it. But if you tell me to stop, it's stopped. Okay?"

Reno found himself rubbing his hand over his brand nervously, a habit he had developed since getting it, to feel the smooth yet raised lines on the skin of his arm, as if afraid it was going to be taken away.

Bounce softened in tone and expression as he watched Reno's nerves spike up and rise from the man's fragile ego. "It's not in the rules because I don't believe any Breaker had even considered doing so. You're fine, Reno."

Bounce glanced around the small place and then back to Reno as he crossed his arms on his chest, causing the chair to let out another moan of protest.

"Well, it should be easy for you to pack." Smirked and pointed a finger to the curtain. "With the exception of that stash, of course. I'll send a Relay from the Grid to deposit that in a bank account for you."

Reno blinked and took a step back in alarm, trying to gulp the feeling down. "Why pack? Where am I going? Look, I've done my job. I don't think I've lost any humans and I kill every night. I don't even take nights off because I need it as much as you need me to do it. If I've broken a rule just tell me and I'll fix it. I don't want to be taken offline."

He whispered and his voice sounded like that of a scared little kid as he met the god's eyes, squeaking out. "Or bounced."

Reno hadn't realized his retreat had continued as he spoke until his back hit the wall behind him. He had been so careful and made sure to obey all the rules as well as not take anything for granted.

Why was he going to be taken off the roster of

Breakers? Where did he screw up?

Bounce could feel Reno's panic mixed with fear so he stood and put a hand up to calm him, as he stowed his shades in his jacket pocket.

"No, Reno. You're still in the system. But it's time you were transferred. You're off probation."

Reno almost slid his ass to the floor in relief to find out he wasn't being taken offline, and would have if not for the wall. But then Bounce's words sank in causing him to give Bounce a frown in confusion.

"Transferred? Where?"

Bounce crossed his arms, leaned back on a heel, and said in a reserved tone, anticipating Reno's reaction. "San Francisco."

He blinked at the god's words and frowned as his eyes drifted right then left and then a few more times both ways. That didn't make any sense did it?

He brought a hand up to run fingers through soft brown hair that never even tried to lie down and always wanted to stick up everywhere as if giving away the mixed up brain it sprouted over.

His too blue gaze came back to look at Bounce and he had to close his mouth to think before he spoke. That was something he wasn't always the best at but this was too important not to find out the right answers by asking the right questions.

"Jess still there?"

Bounce shook his head slowly as he looked away to answer. "No. He left shortly after you were made."

That answer caused Reno to frown more than he already was. Maybe he always avoided the rosters of the other Breakers for that very reason. As much as he and Jess obviously hated each other now there was always that part that remembered when it was just the two of them, the only friend the other one had.

They had been closer than even brothers could be since they shared the same soul, the same head and the same heartache for so long. But that had ended. Maybe Jess found it easy to just move on especially since he thought his former split had been destroyed for the greater good. But Reno wasn't sure if he totally had.

Lowering his head as his chin went to his chest to look at the floor, asked softly, "And her?"

That was the big one.

Emma, the beautiful Witch who had caused the end of his and Jess's communion of destiny together, lived in San Francisco.

That one woman he loved. The only one he had ever been with. Sure he could have as much sex as he wanted and some of the Breakers were regular horn-dogs about it. Women loved the power the Breakers seemed to ooze, even if they didn't know why.

He was constantly getting their attention with his easy going smile and goofy fun manner so he could have had a woman every night just like the rest.

But he didn't because none of them were her.

Bounce swung his gaze back to him, the god's eyes a cool almost ice blue which then darkened like the ocean at night. Gosh, Reno wished he had a chart to tell him what the colors in the god's eyes meant. But there probably wasn't such a cheat tool for they seemed to be ever-changing.

Bounce looked away as he read Reno's thoughts to pull out his shades and slid them on slowly as he spoke softly.

"You said you wanted a new life. One where no one, not even her, knew who you were and did I not indeed grant that?"

Reno swallowed and nodded because it was true. He had been given the option and had chosen it. No one, not Jess, not Emma, no one knew who or what he used to be. Fresh start and one he had a say-so in. "I know. And I mean it. And yes, you did. But uh, is she still there? I just need to know. That's all."

Bounce hissed out a long breath through that perfect nose and nodded before answering. "Yes. She is still there. But Reno?"

The god stepped up and put a hand on his shoulder to look down at him. "There is much pain and heartbreak when it comes to Emma. And Jess. Much you may not want to know or even want brought up. And can you honestly hide the way you feel about her from her? From anyone? Because the feelings you have for her are bright as a spotlight at midnight when you speak of her. Trust me when I say it would be best if you left her alone. Stay away from Emma and out of her life if you truly love her."

Okay, all that was probably true and most likely the best way to handle it.

But Bounce was right about how he felt. Even though it had been three years since he had last seen Emma or Jess, or even been to San Francisco, his heart still ached for her. He still remembered that the last time they had seen each other she had thrown him out of her house for breaking her heart. Sure, she thought he was Jess and probably was never told about the split he used to be, but the sight of her crying and heartbroken still haunted him. He wanted to make her all better and fix whatever Jess had broken.

But while he wasn't the smartest, he also knew that getting involved with her life opened up cans of worms bigger than those cans of cash he had hidden away.

Sighing, he nodded and pulled away from Bounce's hand to walk over to the window to stare at the now pitch black Reno night.

Asked softly, "When do I leave?"

CHAPTER THREE

Emma Devenmore heard maybe half of what the charming man who sat across from her at the dinner table had said. Not bad on the eyes, so much so that the rest of the restaurant kept darting looks at the striking man. But Emma just could not see what the rest in the place saw.

Sure, he was rich, charming, well spoken, nicely dressed and handsome as well as owned one of the top accounting firms in the city.

She seriously suspected he could get any woman he wanted and was doing charity work when her younger sister Lily had set him up on a blind date with her dateless 'for far too long' sister. But Emma found herself completely bored as she smiled and nodded toying with the expensive meal in front of her without taking a bite.

It wasn't his fault, not at all. It was hers.

Because after you had dated an immortal, fang-baring, bad-ass tough, super strong and even sexier than any Greek wannabe god, Breaker, humans just seemed mundane and boring. Add to her still being heartbroken from her last long term, albeit just months, relationship, the guy really didn't stand a chance.

She looked down as he took her hand and then glanced up to meet his eyes. Emma bet he didn't even need those designer glasses but wore them to look more intelligent.

As a healer, she didn't sense anything wrong with the man's vision and she smirked at that. Vanity was something she never had tolerance for. The guy was losing points by the minute and didn't even know he was being graded on a scale he couldn't possibly reach.

"Emma? Didn't you hear me? I would love for you to come back to my place." He brought her hand up to his lips and she stiffened as he kissed her palm, and let his lips linger there.

She smiled and pulled her hand away gently as she looked around and back. How could she say this without coming off as a total bitch?

"No. But thank you?"

Fail, for that seemed to have total ice bitch dripped all over it. His face and eyes showed it and it was easy for Emma to tell he was not a man used to being rejected. Ever.

He gave her a look of shock that affirmed that fact as he raised a brow and said with an edge of arrogance. "Why not?"

She smirked more as she toyed with the bread on her plate, giving a shrug as she answered, lifting her eyes to his.

"To be honest? You're boring."

She stood up, swinging on her jacket as she pulled her purse off the back of her chair to look back at his shocked did-you-really face.

"And chances are? You aren't any better in bed. Sorry."

He just gawked as she walked out into the cool, fog dripping air of San Francisco. She could have handled that better, but she had just had no inclination to do so. She had been on three dates since breaking up with Jess and all three had the same outcome. Different men, indifferent feelings and wanting something more.

It wasn't that she wasn't ready to move on and even fall in love again. She ached for it. But no one felt right. No one made her feel like she did with Jess.

As she tied the belt of her coat to wrap it tight around her, eyes down to stare at the sidewalk under her shoes as she headed for the Bayside Park, she knew that wasn't the total truth.

The whole time she and Jess had been together she had craved and ached for something then too.

The same feeling she had that first night they had spent together and made love for the first time. It had been so genuine and real, honest and the most emotional she had ever felt from the man with whom she spent almost five months of her life. The whole time they were together, she kept seeking that same connection and closeness she had felt that one night.

There were times when it seemed so close but always fell short. She knew it and sadly, so did Jess. But whereas it made her sad and long for it, whenever she voiced it or wondered out loud, it made Jess angry.

That never made any sense to Emma but every time she brought it up to discuss or even talk about it, it would launch them into an argument or screaming match.

Finally Emma had just given up seeking that sensation of magic and specialness of their first night together, and threw herself into loving what had come out of it.

But something never seemed right between them, no matter the love they felt for each other, and it finally had to be faced. They had tried so hard to stay together until the very end. But it had all been for nothing.

Well, not for nothing.

For one reason and one reason only, she was glad they had what they did. That one very precious thing was worth it all and she would never change or take back.

But even now, she still wished some nights, to just feel like she did that one night. Maybe it had been a dream, just like the one that repeated over and over in her mind as she slept. Maybe, it had all just been her imagination and she was a fool to crave something that wasn't even real.

It was the scent of vanilla that hit Reno's senses first, causing his head to snap up to stop him walking in his tracks.

Long dark hair, curling in the fog as it lifted in the breeze, around a beautiful face with eyes cast down so he couldn't see.

Long legs in strappy heels below a sweet body he still remembered as clear as if yesterday. The memory of it and their night together were grounds for some hand to happy part, so many times. She was shrouded in a coat against the night and seemed deep in thought. But he didn't need to see her face to know it was her.

Emma. His Witch.

Reno's first instinct was to run and not let her see him until he remembered he was in a new body with a new face; there was no way she could recognize him.

He had been on patrol for Eaters when he decided a walk by the Bay would be a nice break from not finding anything to kill. Anytime he didn't find any prey, his head would get buzzing like a thousand bees to satisfy the need for pain and violence. If it got too bad, not even candy would help and he would have to go home and do some damage working out, cutting his own flesh or hitting the wall.

Once again, his gift for bad decisions was making itself known as one of the two people whom he should really avoid was walking towards him and he was hoping she got closer, despite his logic telling him that was not a good idea.

Putting his head down as he shoved his hands in his pockets, turned his head to watch her walk by with a sideways glance with their shoulders just inches apart.

Closing his eyes, his nostrils flared to breathe her in and Reno's body had the same soar of arousal it had with just a thought of her when he was alone.

He was so caught up in it that he didn't realize she had stopped to stare at him. His eyes snapped open and he looked forward, licking his suddenly dried lips and telling his stupid legs to get moving when she said something soft and sweet.

"Do I know you?"

He did an internal wince as he kept his back to her but shook his head, digging his fingers into his palms as they fisted in his pockets.

There was no way she could know. No way had she known who he was then or now, because she never knew him at all. He had never really existed for her. But god, did he want to exist with her but it was a really, really bad idea. The worst idea, ever.

Reno wanted to say "yes, and I love you". To tell her he dreamed of her every day and thought of her every night. But his common sense actually had its way. Maybe the only time it ever had or ever would.

"No."

Emma stared at his back for the longest time, and for a minute there, though he knew his senses told him differently, Reno thought she had left.

He looked over his shoulder back at her with his blue eyes meeting her beautiful green ones and he lost his breath. God, she was just as beautiful as she had been going on almost four years since the last time he had seen her. His eyes darted to her lips without even asking his brain permission and he swallowed down a throat that was suddenly dry as if thirsty.

Emma had no idea why she felt some strange attraction to this man in the park who was a total stranger and she felt confused.

Maybe it was because he was good looking in an almost boyish way. With eyes that were a piercing blue which seemed to spark with so much more going on behind them. He was tall, but shorter than a Breaker with this unruly soft brown, wavy hair that didn't seem to want to behave. Add to that broad shoulders, tapered waist and long legs which she bet he just owned naturally by good genetics and not days at the gym. Or hotter, more intense exercises that involved the bed, a kitchen counter or maybe a wall.

But there was something more beyond the physical attraction. Emma dealt with gorgeous men every day working for the Grid.

No, it was like Emma knew him and she knew that was completely ridiculous.

They were strangers and despite his quiet almost forced response of no, she felt like the answer should have been yes. She was even more baffled to realize she wanted it to be yes and knew that no was wrong.

They must have stood there for what seemed like hours when in reality it was only half a minute.

Reno turned away to face forward to finally get his feet to move as he walked into the fog, leaving her standing there to watch him go and had no idea how he had the strength to do it. Reno continued to walk away and he knew it was the hardest thing he had ever had to do.

Leaving Emma standing there, unable to move from the spot with a sense of panic to stop a stranger and beg him not to go.

THE GRID GLOSSARY

**There are many types of beings on the Grid.
Here are just a few:**

Breakers: Supernatural heroes with a dark past. For the price a coin containing their soul, they are bought from Hell by Bounce to become part of the Grid where they fight the darkness and destroy the demons from Hell, called Eaters. If they do their job well, when the war ends, or they find love, they get a second chance at life if found worthy and obtain both freedom and immortality for themselves and those they love.

Relays: Human and other counterparts of the Grid. There are several kinds just as with any army.

Tech Relays: The computer and technical side of the Grid. They monitor and maintain the vast Grid located in Fort Pearce under the Golden Gate Bridge. Techs have limited fighting skills but incredible analytical abilities.

Recon Relays: The human counterparts who are trained to have both fighting and tactical skills as well as trained as snipers. Recon Relays are the ones who hunt down those wishing to destroy or harm the Grid on the inside.

Wires: The top of the human Recon food chain, these human counterparts go through an intense testing process to prove they are the best of all the humans that fight on the Grid.

Healer Relays: Humans and deities who serve to heal those on the Grid. Gifted with the talent of touch-electrotherapy, they can access their spark to heal another. If they tap too much, their spark goes dark, and they die.

Bridge Relays: The engineers of the Grid who not only worked closely with Tesla in its design but are constantly designing new technology to ensure it stays ahead of the war and to assist those on the Grid.

Municipal (Muni) Relays: These are humans who work for the various branches of government and agencies in the city. They are aware of the Grid and use their positions to keep it hidden. Some examples include deputy mayor, police officers, and firemen.

Other Designation: This designation is for other beings on The Grid with no standard classification.

Vampire: Not part of the Grid but working closely with Bounce and the High Council to   align the two races and armies. Based in New Orleans.

Shadow-Keepers:

Known as Keepers, they are at the top of the food chain on the Grid. These beings are animated by the dark power that must exist to keep the balance of dark and light. The Keepers walk the shadow in between by feeding their powers while keeping them controlled so the darkness never overcomes and destroys the light.

Reno Sundown: Keeper of Madness and former Breaker on the Grid. The first Keeper created by Epsilon, son of Lucifer.

Make sure you join the reader and character interaction group on Facebook. Not only can you chat with Ward, but you can also discuss with some of the characters you met in this book!

Yes, even Reno.

Join it here:

http://bit.ly/GridNightsFandom

And if you want to dive into another Ward World, check out her Soul Bound Trilogy.

You can find Book I: The Warrior here –

https://books2read.com/SoulBoundOne

Be warned, you may not survive the read.

#SBSurviveTheRead

Join Ward's Newsletter here for exclusive FIRST LOOKS & Other Member Exclusive Content:

www.AuthorJasTWard.com

ALSO WRITTEN BY JAS T. WARD

Poetry & Short Stories
Bits & Pieces

Dark Paranormal Romance

The Grid Series
Reading Order
Candyman: Book One
Madness: Book Two
Bounce: Book Three
Lust: Book Four
Cowboy: Book Five
Murder: Book Six
Envy: Book Seven
Hostage: Spin-Off*
Chaos: Book Eight
Sundown: The Final

* K. Bromberg's
Everyday Heroes World

The Soul Bound Trilogy
Reading Order
The Warrior: Book One
The Wounded: Book Two
The Wanted: Book Three

Contemporary Romance (Standalones)
A Little Pill Called Love
Love's Bitter Harvest

ABOUT THE AUTHOR

"I am the product of several realities making the whole: a troubled childhood, domestic violence survivor, homeless person, single mother and a murder/suicide survivor. But in every single one of those realities, one thing remained true - my imagination."

Reading and writing has always been Ms. Ward's escape. And she wants to continue to give that to her readers as well. Known for action, drama, laughter, darkness and twists you don't see coming in the same book, Ward is known for writing books that are diverse, different and unique. A bestselling author on both Amazon and ARe Romance, Ms. Ward's books have won awards from various blogs and Preditors and Editors in the categories of reader favorites, best dark romance and others. Ms. Ward's books have also been reviewed in Ind'Tale Magazine and been nominated for their prestigious RONE awards for each time a finalist.

Born and raised in Texas and spending time living in Kentucky, Ms. Ward spends her days and nights writing as therapy to deal with life and all that it brings—from the past and present. And hopefully finds joy, laughter and fun to mix in with the dark. Something her readers have come to love in her works. She is the proud parent of three very independent grown children and grandmother to three delightful grandchildren. She has two fur babies that sit and ponder why their human is talking to herself late into the night as she writes out colorful and diverse if not twisted characters and tales.

Links so we can keep in touch.

Website: www.AuthorJasTWard.com
You can sign up for my newsletter and get a free read!